Look Back on Happiness

Knut Hamsun

Look Back on Happiness

ISBN: 978-1-63637-739-1

LOOK BACK ON HAPPINESS

I

I have gone to the forest.

Not because I am offended about anything, or very unhappy about men's evil ways; but since the forest will not come to me, I must go to it. That is all. I have not gone this time as a slave and a vagabond. I have money enough and am overfed, stupefied with success and good fortune, if you understand that. I have left the world as a sultan leaves rich food and harems and flowers, and clothes himself in a hair shirt.

Really, I could make quite a song and dance about it. For I mean to roam and think and make great irons red-hot. Nietzsche no doubt would have spoken thus: The last word I spake unto men achieved their praise, and they nodded. But it was my last word; and I went into the forest. For then did I comprehend the truth, that my speech must needs be dishonest or foolish.... But I said nothing of the kind; I simply went to the forest.

You must not believe that nothing ever happens here. The snowflakes drift down just as they do in the city, and the birds and beasts scurry about from morning till night, and from night till morning. I could send solemn stories from this place, but I do not. I have sought the forest for solitude and for the sake of my great irons; for I have great irons which lie within me and grow red-hot. So I deal with myself accordingly. Suppose I were to meet a buck reindeer one day, then I might say to myself:

"Great heavens, this is a buck reindeer, he's dangerous!"

But if then I should be too frightened, I might tell myself a comforting lie and say it was a calf or some feathered beast.

You say nothing happens here?

1

One day I saw two Lapps meet. A boy and a girl. At first they behaved as people do. "Boris!" they said to each other and smiled. But immediately after, both fell at full length in the snow and were gone from my sight. After a quarter of an hour had passed, I thought, "You'd better see to them; they may be smothered in the snow." But then they got up and went their separate ways.

In all my weatherbeaten days, I have never seen such a greeting as that.

Day and night I live in a deserted hut of peat into which I must crawl on my hands and knees. Someone must have built it long ago and used it, for lack of a better,—perhaps a man who was in hiding, a man who concealed himself here for a few autumn days. There are two of us in the hut, that is if you regard Madame as a person; otherwise there is only one. Madame is a mouse I live with, to whom I have given this honorary title. She eats everything I put aside for her in the nooks and corners, and sometimes she sits watching me.

When I first came, there was stale straw in the hut, which Madame by all means was allowed to keep; for my own bed I cut fresh pine twigs, as is fitting. I have an ax and a saw and the necessary crockery. And I have a sleeping bag of sheepskin with the wool inside. I keep a fire burning in the fireplace all night, and my shirt, which hangs by it, smells of fresh resin in the morning. When I want coffee, I go out, fill the kettle with clean snow, and hang it over the fire till the snow turns to water.

Is this a life worth living?

There you have betrayed yourself. This is a life you do not understand. Yes, your home is in the city, and you have furnished it with vanities, with pictures and books; but you have a wife and a servant and a hundred expenses. Asleep or awake you must keep pace with the world and are never at peace. I have peace. You are welcome to your intellectual pastimes and books and art and newspapers; welcome, too, to your bars and your whisky that only makes me ill. Here am I in the forest, quite content. If you ask me intellectual questions and try to trip me up, then I will reply, for example, that God is the origin of all things and that truly men are mere specks and atoms in the universe. You are no wiser than I. But if you should go so far as to ask me what is eternity, then I know quite as much in this matter, too, and reply thus: Eternity is merely unborn time, nothing but unborn time.

My friend, come here to me and I will take a mirror from my pocket and reflect the sun on your face, my friend.

You lie in bed till ten or eleven in the morning, yet you are weary, exhausted, when you get up. I see you in my mind's eye as you go out into the street; the morning has dawned too early on your blinking eyes. I rise at five quite refreshed. It is still dark outdoors, yet there is enough to look at—the moon, the stars, the clouds, and the weather portents for the day. I prophesy the weather for many hours ahead. In what key do the winds whistle? Is the crack of the ice in the Glimma light and dry, or deep and long? These are splendid portents, and as it grows lighter, I add the visible signs to the audible ones, and learn still more.

Then a narrow streak of daylight appears far down in the east, the stars fade from the sky, and soon light reigns over all. A crow flies over the woods, and I warn Madame not to go outside the hut or she will be devoured.

But if fresh snow has fallen, the trees and copses and the great rocks take on giant, unearthly shapes, as though they had come from another world in the night. A storm-felled pine with its root torn up looks like a witch petrified in the act of performing strange rites.

Here a hare has sprung by, and yonder are the tracks of a solitary reindeer. I shake out my sleeping bag and after hanging it high in a tree to escape Madame, who eats everything, I follow the tracks of the reindeer into the forest. It has jogged along without haste, but toward a definite goal—straight east to meet the day. By the banks of the Skiel, which is so rapid that its waters never freeze, the reindeer has stopped to drink, to scrape the hillside for moss, to rest a while, and then moved on.

And perhaps what this reindeer has done is all the knowledge and experience I gain that day. It seems much to me. The days are short; at two, I am already strolling homeward in the deep twilight, with the good, still night approaching. Then I begin to cook. I have a great deal of meat stored in three pure-white drifts of snow. In fact I have something even better: eight fat cheeses of reindeer milk, to eat with butter and crisp-bread.

While the pot is boiling I lie down, and gaze at the fire till I fall asleep. I take my midday nap before my meal. And when I waken, the food is cooked, filling the hut with an aroma of meat and resin.

3

Madame darts back and forth across the floor and at length gets her share. I eat, and light my cutty-pipe.

The day is at an end. All has been well, and I have had no unpleasantness. In the great silence surrounding me, I am the only adult, roaming man; this makes me bigger and more important, God's kin. And I believe the red-hot irons within me are progressing well, for God does great things for his kin.

I lie thinking of the reindeer, the path it took, what it did by the river, and how it continued on its journey. There under the trees it has nibbled, and its horns have rubbed against the bark, leaving their marks; there an osier bed has forced it to turn aside; but just beyond, it has straightened its path and continued east once more. All this I think of.

And you? Have you read in a newspaper, which disagrees with another newspaper, what the public in Norway is thinking of old-age insurance?

II

On stormy days I sit indoors and find something to occupy my time. Perhaps I write letters to some acquaintance or other telling him I am well, and hope to hear the same from him. But I cannot post the letters, and they grow older every day. Not that it matters. I have tied the letters to a string that hangs from the ceiling to prevent Madame from gnawing at them.

One day a man came to the hut. He walked swiftly and stealthily; his clothes were ordinary and he wore no collar, for he was a laboring man. He carried a sack, and I wondered what could be in it.

"Good morning," we said to each other. "Fine weather in the woods."

"I didn't expect to find anybody in the hut," said the man. His manner was at once forceful and discontented; he flung down the sack without humility.

"He may know something about me," I thought, "since he is such a man."

"Have you lived here long?" he asked. "And are you leaving soon?"

"Is the hut yours, perhaps?" I asked in my turn.

Then he looked at me.

"Because if the hut is yours, that's another matter," I said. "But I don't intend like a pickpocket to take it with me when I leave."

I spoke gently and jestingly to avoid committing a blunder by my speech.

But I had said quite the right thing; the man at once lost his assurance. Somehow I had made him feel that I knew more about him than he knew about me.

When I asked him to come in, he was grateful and said:

"Thank you, but I'm afraid I'll get snow all over your floor."

Then he took special pains to wipe his boots clean, and bringing his sack with him, crawled in.

"I could give you some coffee," I said.

"You shouldn't trouble on my account," he replied, wiping his face and panting with the heat, "though I've been walking all night."

"Are you crossing the fjeld?"

"That depends. I don't suppose there's work to be got on a winter day on the other side, either."

I gave him coffee.

"Got anything to eat?" he said. "It's a shame to ask you. A round of crisp-bread? I had no chance to bring food with me."

"Yes, I've got bread, butter, and reindeer cheese. Help yourself."

"It's not so easy for a lot of people in the winter," said the man as he ate.

"Could you take some letters to the village for me?" I asked. "I'll pay you for it."

"Oh, no, I couldn't do that," the man replied. "I'm afraid that's impossible. I must cross the fjeld now. I've heard there's work in Hilling, in the Hilling Forest. So I can't."

"Must get his back up a bit again," I thought. "He just sits now there without any guts at all. In the end he'll start begging for a few coppers."

I felt his sack and said:

"What's this you're lugging about with you? Heavy things?"

"Mind your own business!" was his instant retort, as he drew the sack closer to him.

"I wasn't going to steal any of it; I'm no thief," I said, jesting again.

"I don't care what you are," he muttered.

The day wore on. Since I had a visitor, I had no desire to go to the woods, but wanted to sit and talk to him and ask him questions. He was a very ordinary man, of no great interest to the irons in my fire, with dirty hands, uneducated and uninteresting in his speech; probably he had stolen the things in his sack. Later I learned that he was quick in much small knowledge that life had taught him. He complained that his heels felt cold, and took off his boots. And no wonder he felt cold, for where the heels of his stockings should have been there were only great holes. He borrowed a knife to cut away the ragged edges, and then drew on the stockings again back to front, so that the torn soles came over his instep. When he had put on his boots again, he said, "There, now it's nice and warm."

He did no harm. If he took down the saw and the ax from their hooks to inspect them, he put them back again where he had found them. When he examined the letters, trying perhaps to read the addresses, he did not let them go carelessly, leaving them to swing back and forth, but held the string so that it hung motionless. I had no reason to complain about him.

He had his midday meal with me, and when he had eaten, he said:

"Do you mind if I cut myself some pine twigs to sit on?"

He went out to cut off some soft pine, and we had to move Madame's straw to make room for the man inside the hut. Then we lay on our twigs, burning resin and talking.

6

He was still there in the afternoon, still lying down as though to postpone the time of his leaving. When it began to grow dark, he went to the low doorway and looked out at the weather. Then, turning his head back, he asked:

"Do you think there'll be snow tonight?"

"You ask me questions and I ask you questions," I said, "but it looks like snow; the smoke is blowing down."

It made him uneasy to think it might snow, and he said he had better leave that night. Suddenly he flew into a rage. For as I lay there, I stretched, so that my hand accidentally touched his sack again.

"You leave me alone!" he shouted, tearing the sack from my grasp. "Don't you touch that sack, or I'll show you!"

I replied that I had meant nothing by it, and had no intention of stealing anything from him.

"Stealing, eh! What of it? I'm not afraid of you, and don't you go thinking I am! Look, here's what I've got in the bag," said the man, and began to rummage in it and to show me the contents: three pairs of new mittens, some sort of thick cloth for garments, a bag of barley, a side of bacon, sixteen rolls of tobacco, and a few large lumps of sugar candy. In the bottom of the bag was perhaps half a bushel of coffee beans.

No doubt it was all from the general stores, with the exception of a heap of broken crisp-bread, which might have been stolen elsewhere.

"So you've got crisp-bread after all," I said.

"If you knew anything about it, you wouldn't talk like that," the man replied. "When I'm crossing the fjeld on foot, walking and walking, don't I need food to put in my belly? It's blasphemy to listen to you!"

Neatly and carefully he put everything back into the sack, each article in its turn. He took pains to build up the rolls of tobacco round the bacon, to protect the cloth from grease stains.

"You might buy this cloth from me," he said. "I'll

let you have it cheap. It's duffle. It only gets in my way."

"How much do you want for it?" I asked.

"There's enough for a whole suit of clothes, maybe more," he said to himself as he spread it out.

I said to the man:

"Truly you come here into the forest bringing with you life and the world and intellectual values and news. Let us talk a little. Tell me something: are you afraid your footprints will be visible tomorrow if there's fresh snow tonight?"

"That's my business. I've crossed the field before and I know many paths," he muttered. "I'll let you have the cloth for a few crowns."

I shook my head, so the man again neatly folded the cloth and put it back in the bag exactly as though it belonged to him.

"I'll cut it up into material for trousers; then the pieces won't be so large, and I'll be able to sell it."

"You'd better leave enough for a whole suit in one piece," I said, "and cut up the rest for trousers."

"You think so? Yes, maybe you're right."

We calculated how much would be necessary for a grown man's suit, and took down the string from which the letters hung to measure our own clothes, so as to be sure to get the measurements right. Then we cut into the edge of the cloth, and tore it across. In addition to one complete suit, there was enough left for two good-sized pairs of trousers.

Then the man offered to sell me other things out of his sack, and I bought some coffee and a few rolls of tobacco. He put the money away in a leather purse, and I saw how empty the purse was, and the circumstantial and poverty-stricken fashion in which he put the money away, afterward feeling the outside of his pocket.

"You haven't been able to sell me much," I said, "but I don't need any more than that."

"Business is business," said he. "I don't complain."

It was quite decent of him.

While he was making ready to depart and clearing his bed of pine

8

needles out of the way, I thought pityingly of his sordid little theft. Stealing because he was needy—a side of bacon and a length of cloth which he was trying to sell in the forest! Theft has indeed ceased to be a matter of great moment. This is because legal punishment for misdemeanors of all kinds has also ceased to be of great moment. It is only a dull, human punishment; the religious element has been removed from the law, and a local magistrate is no longer a man of mystic power.

I well remember the last time I heard a judge explain the meaning of the oath as it should be explained. It chilled us all to the bone to hear him. We need some witchcraft again, and the Sixth Book of Moses, and the sin against the Holy Ghost, and signing your name in the blood of a newly baptized child! Steal a sack of money and silver treasure, if you like, and hide the sack in the hills where on autumn evenings a blue flame will hover over the spot. But don't come to me with three pairs of mittens and a side of household bacon!

The man no longer worried about the sack; leaving it behind, he crawled out of the hut to study the weather. The coffee and tobacco I had bought I put back into the sack, for I did not need them. When he returned, he said:

"I think after all I'd better stop the night here with you, if you don't mind."

In the evening he gave no indication of being prepared to contribute any of his own food. I cooked some coffee and gave him some dry bread to eat with it.

"You shouldn't have expenses for me," he said.

Then he began to rummage in his sack again, pushing the bacon well down so that the cloth might not be stained by it; after this he took off his leather belt and put it round the sack, with a loop to carry over one shoulder.

"Now if I take the neck of the sack over the other shoulder, I'll find it easier to carry," he said.

I gave him my letters to post on the other side of the fjeld and he stowed them away safely, slapping the outside of his pocket afterward; I also gave him a special envelope in which to keep the money for the stamps, and tied it to the neck of the sack.

"Where do you live?" I asked him.

"Where can a poor man live? Of course I live by the sea. I'm sorry to say I have a wife and children—no use denying it."

"How many children have you?"

"Four. One's got a crippled arm and the others—there's something wrong with all of them. It's not easy for a poor devil. My wife's ill, and a few days ago she thought she was dying and wanted Communion."

A sad note crept into his voice. But the note was false. He was telling me a pack of lies. When they came to look for him from the village, no Christian would have the heart to accuse a man with such a large and sick family. This, no doubt, was his meaning.

Man, oh man, thou art worse than a mouse!

I questioned him no further, but asked him to sing something, a ballad or a song, since we had nothing else to do.

"I've no heart to sing now," he replied. "Except possibly a hymn."

"All right; sing a hymn, then."

"Not now. I'd like to do you a favor, but—"

His uneasiness was rising. A little later he took his sack and went out.

"Well, he's gone," I thought, "but he hasn't said the customary peace-be-with-you. I'm glad I've come into the forest," I thought. "This is my home, and from this day forth, no mother's son shall come within my walls again."

I made an elaborate agreement with myself that I should have no more truck with men.

"Madame, come here," I said. "I esteem you highly, and herewith, Madame, I undertake to enter upon a union with you for life!"

Half an hour later, the man returned. He carried no sack.

"I thought you'd gone," I said.

"Gone? I'm not a dog," he replied. "I've met people before this, and I

10

say good morning when I come and peace-be-with-you when I go. You shouldn't sneer at me, you know."

"What have you done with the sack?"

"I've carried it part of the way."

His concealing the sack in case anyone should come proved he had forethought, for it was easier to get away scot-free without a burden on one's back. To stop him from telling me any more lies about his poverty, I said:

"I expect you've raised plenty of dust in your day? Still do, for that matter?"

"Well, I do what I can," he replied cheerfully. "I can lift a barrel easier than most, and nobody was able to dance me off the floor last Christmas! Hush—is that someone coming?"

We listened. His eyes darted toward the entrance, and in a moment he had chosen to meet danger halfway. He was taut and splendid; I could see his jaw working.

"It's nothing," I said.

Resolute and strong as a bull, he crawled out of the hut and was gone for a few minutes. When he returned, breathing heavily, he said:

"It's nothing."

We lay down for the night.

"In God's name!" he said, as he settled himself on his pine bed. I fell asleep at once, and for some time slept deeply. But during the night restlessness seized on the man again. "Peace be with you!" I heard him mutter as he crawled out of the hut.

In the morning I burned the man's bed of pine needles; it made a lively fire of crackling pine in the hut.

Outside, the ground was covered with new-fallen snow.

III

There is nothing like being left alone again, to walk peacefully with oneself in the woods. To boil one's coffee and fill one's pipe, and to think idly and slowly as one does it.

There, now I'll fill the kettle with snow, I think, and now I'm crushing the coffee beans with a stone; later I must beat my sleeping bag well in the snow and get the wool white again. There is nothing in this of literature or great novels or public opinion; does it matter? But then I haven't been toiling just to get this coffee into my life. Literature? When Rome ruled the world, she was no more than Greece's apprentice in literature. Yet Rome ruled the world. Let us look too at another country we know: it fought a war of independence the glory of which still shines, and it brought forth the greatest school of painting in the world. Yet it had no literature, and has none today....

Day by day I grow more knowing in the ways of the trees and the moss and the snow on the ground, and all things are my friends. The stump of a fir tree stands thawing in the sun; I feel my familiarity with it grow, and sometimes I stand there loving it, for there is something in it that moves my soul. The bark is badly broken. One winter in the deep snow, the tree must have been crippled, and now it points upward long and naked. I put myself in its place, and look at it with pity. My eyes perhaps have the simple, animal expression that human eyes had in the age of the mastodons.

No doubt you will seize this opportunity to mock me, for there are many amusing things you can say about me and this stump of a fir. Yet in your heart, you know that I am superior to you in this as in everything else, with the single exception that I have not your conventional accomplishments, nor have I passed examinations. About the forest and the earth you can teach me nothing, for here I feel what no man else has felt.

Sometimes I take the wrong direction and lose my way. Yes, truly this may happen sometimes. But I do not begin to twist and lose myself outside my very door, like the children of the city. I am twelve miles out, far up the opposite bank of the Skjel River, before I begin to get lost, and then only on a sunless day, with perhaps thick, wild snow coming down, and no north or south in the sky. Then you must know the special marks of this kind of tree and that, the galipot of the pine, the bark of deciduous trees, the moss that grows at their roots, the angle of the south and north-pointing branches, the stones that are moss-covered and those that are bare, and the pattern of the network of veins in the leaves. From all these things while there is daylight I can find my way.

But if the dusk falls, I know it will be impossible for me to get home till the next day. "How shall I pass this night?" I say to myself. And I roam about till I find a sheltered spot; the best is a crag standing with its back to the wind. Here I collect a few armfuls of pine needles, button my jacket tight, and take a long time to settle. No one who has not tried it knows anything of the fine pleasure that streams through the soul as one sits in a snug shelter on such a night. I light my pipe to pass the time, but the tobacco doesn't agree with me because I haven't eaten, so I put some resin in my mouth to chew as I lie thinking of many things. The snow continues to fall outside; if I have been lucky enough to find a shelter facing the right way, the snowdrifts will close in over me and form a crest like a roof above my retreat. Then I am quite safe, and may sleep or wake as I please; there will be no danger of freezing my feet.

Two men came to my hut; they were in a great hurry, and one of them called to me:

"Good morning. Has a man passed this way?"

I didn't like his face. I was not his servant and his question was too stupid.

"Many people may have passed this way. Do you mean have I seen a man go by?"

So much for him!

"I meant what I said," the man replied surlily. "I'm asking you in the name of the law."

"Oh."

I had no desire for further conversation, and crawled into my hut.

The two men followed me. The constable grinned and said:

"Did you see a man pass by here yesterday?"

"No," I said.

They looked at each other, and took counsel together; then they left the hut and returned to the village.

I thought: What zeal this policeman showed in the execution of his duties, how he shone with public spirit! There will be bonuses for the capture and transport of the criminal; there will be honor in having carried out the deed. All mankind should adopt this man because he is its son, created in its image! Where are the irons? He would rattle the links a little and lift them on his arm like the train of a riding skirt, to make me feel his terrifying power to put people in irons ... I feel nothing.

And what tradesmen—what kings of trade—we have today! They instantly miss what a man can carry off in a sack, and notify the police.

From now on I begin to long for the spring. My peat hut lies still too near to mankind, and I will build myself another when the frost has gone out of the ground. On the other side of the Skjel, I have chosen a spot in the forest which I think I shall like. It is twenty-four miles from the village and eighteen across the fjeld.

IV

Have I said that I was too near men? Heaven help me, for some days in succession I have been taking strolls in the forest, saying good morning and pretending I was in human company. If it was a man I imagined beside me, we carried on a long, intelligent conversation, but if it was a woman, I was polite: "Let me carry your parcel, miss." Once it must have been the Lapp's daughter I seemed to meet, for I flattered her most lavishly and offered to carry her fur cloak if she would take it off and walk in her skin; tut, tut.

Heaven help me, I am no longer too near men. And probably I will not build that peat hut still further away from them.

The days grow longer, and I do not mind. The truth is that in the winter I suffered privation and learned much in order to master myself. It has taken time and sometimes a resolute will, so it cannot be denied that I am paying for my education rather dearly. Sometimes I have been needlessly stern with myself.

"There is a loaf of bread," I said. "It doesn't surprise me, it doesn't interest me; I am used to it. But if you see no bread for twelve hours, it will mean something to you," I said, and hid the bread away.

That was in the winter.

Were they dreary days? No, good days. My liberty was so great that I could do and think as I pleased; I was alone, the bear of the forest. But even in the heart of the forest no man dares speak aloud without looking round; rather, he walks in silence. For a time you console yourself that it's typically English to be silent, it's regal to be silent. But suddenly you find this has gone too far, your mouth begins to wake, to stretch, and suddenly to shout nonsense.

"Bricks for the palace! The calf is much stronger today!"

Perhaps if your voice is strong, the sound will carry for a quarter of a mile—but then you feel a sting as though after a slap. If only you had kept your regal silence! One day the postman who crosses the fjeld once a month came on me just as I had shouted.

"What?" he called from the wood.

"Careful below!" I called back to save my face. "I've put out a trap."

But with the longer days, my courage grows; it must be the spring that causes this mysterious revival within me, and I no longer fear a shout more or less. I needlessly rattle my pots and pans as I cook, and I sing at the top of my voice. It is spring.

Yesterday I stood on a hillock and looked out across the wintry woods. They have a different expression now; they have gone gray and bedraggled, and the midday sun has thawed down the snow and diminished it. There are catkins everywhere, drifts of them in the underbrush, looking like letters of the alphabet piled in a heap. The moon rises, the stars break forth. I am cold and shiver a little, but I have nothing to do in the hut, and prefer to shiver as long as possible. In the winter I did nothing so foolish, but went home if I was cold. Now I'm tired of that, too. It is the spring.

The sky is pure and cool, lying wide open to all the stars. There is a great flock of worlds up in that endless meadow, tiny, teeming worlds, so tiny that they are like the sound of a tinkling bell; as I look at them, I can hear thousands of tiny bells. Yes, certainly I am being drawn more and more toward the grassy slopes of spring.

V

I fill the fireplace with pine wood, hoist my belongings to my back, and leave the hut. "Farewell, Madame."

That was the end.

I feel no pleasure at leaving my shelter, but a touch of sadness—as I always do on leaving a place that has been my home for some time. But all the world stands outside calling to me. Indeed I am like all lovers of the woods and fields; wordlessly we had agreed to meet, and as I sat there last night, I felt my eyes being drawn to the door.

Several times I look back at the hut, with the smoke rising up from the chimney; the smoke billows and waves to me, and I wave back.

The silky pallor of the morning refreshes me; in a long blue haze over the forest, a slow dawn rises. It looks like a cheerful piratical coast in the sky before me. The mountains are all on my left.

After a few hours' march I am like new from top to toe, and I press on swiftly. I beat the air with my stick, and it says "hoo" as it swishes; whenever I think I deserve it, I sit down and give myself food.

No, you have not my pleasures in the town.

I beat my legs with my stick from the sheer exuberance of living, and nearly cry out. I behave as though the burden on my back had no weight, taking needless leaps, and overexerting myself a little; but an overexertion to which one is driven by inner content is easy to bear. In my solitude, many miles from men and houses, I am in a childishly happy and carefree state of mind, which you are incapable of understanding unless someone explains it to you. I play a little game with myself, pretending to have discovered a remarkable kind of tree. At first I pay little attention, then I stretch my neck and contract my eyelids and gaze.

"What!" I say to myself. "Surely it couldn't be—"

I throw down my burden and approach, inspect the tree and nod sagely, saying it is a strange, fabled tree that I have discovered. And I take out my notebook and describe it.

16

Merely jest and happiness, a queer little impulse to play. Children have done it before me. And here comes no postman to surprise me. As suddenly as I have begun the game, I end it again, as children do. But for a moment I was transported back to the dear, foolish bliss of childhood.

Perhaps it was the anticipation of soon seeing men again that made me playful and happy!

Next day, just as a raw mist descends on mountain and forest, I reach the Lapp's house. I enter. But though I meet with nothing but kindness, a Lapp hut contains little that is interesting. There are spoons and knives of bone on the peat wall, and a small paraffin lamp hangs from the roof. The Lapp himself is a dull nonentity who can neither tell fortunes nor conjure. His daughter has gone across the field; she has learned to read, but not to write, at the village school. The two old people, husband and wife, are fools. The whole family share a sort of animal dumbness; if I ask them a question, I may or may not get half a reply: "Mm-no, mm-yes." I am not a Lapp, and so they distrust me.

All the afternoon the mist lay white on the forest. I slept a while. In the evening, the sky was clear again, and there were a few degrees of frost. I left the hut. The moon stood full and silent above the earth.

Heigh-ho—what untuned strings!

> But where are the birds all gone away,
> and what kind of place is this?
> Here where I stand nothing moves or stirs,
> in this world that is dead, no event occurs;
> I stand in a silvermine.
> My eyes sweep round, but I sorely miss
> a homely, well-known outline.
>
> And so he came to a silver wood—
> thus ran an ancient tale.
> Here rests a song of shimmering fire
> as though it were sung by a starry choir.
> And swift in my youth, I leap
> to bind fast the troll, the cunning male,
> and awaken a maid from her sleep.
>
> Today I smile at childish tales,
> old age has made me wise.

Once proudly in prodigal youth I trod,
now by age my foot is heavily shod;
yet my heart—my heart would fly.
I am driven by fire and bound by ice,
no rest nor repose have I.

A shuddering chill falls on the night,
like a cloud from the lungs in the cold.
There passed a great gust through the silver lace
of the woods, like a lion's royal pace
on paws that are soundless and still.
It may be a god on his evening stroll.
The roots of the forest thrill.

When I returned to the hut, the daughter had also returned home, and sat eating after her long march. Olga the Lapp, tiny and queer, conceived in a snowdrift, in the course of a greeting. "Boris!" they said and fell on their noses.

She had bought red and blue pieces of cloth at the draper's shop in the village, and no sooner had she finished eating than she pushed the cups and plates away and began to embroider her Sunday jacket with pretty strips of the cloth. All the while she never spoke a word, because a stranger was in the room.

"You know me, Olga, don't you?"

"Mm."

"But you look so angry."

"M-no."

"How's the snow track across the fjeld?"

"All right."

I knew there was a deserted hut the family had once lived in, and asked:

"How far is it to your old hut?"

"Not far," said Olga.

Olga Lapp has someone to smile at surely, even if she will not smile at me. Here she sits in the great forest, pandering to her vanity and sewing wonderful scrolls on her jacket. On Sunday, no doubt, she will wear it to church and meet the man whose eyes it is meant to gladden.

I was not anxious to stay any longer with these small beings, these human grains of sand. As I had slept enough in the afternoon and the moon was bright, I prepared to leave. After laying in a further supply of reindeer cheese and whatever other food I could get, I left the hut. But what a surprise: the bright moonlight was gone, and the sky was overcast; there was no frost, only mild weather and wet woods. It was spring.

When Olga Lapp saw this, she advised me against leaving; but why should I listen to her chatter? She came with me a little way into the woods to direct me, then turned and went back, tiny and queer, her feathers ruffled like a hen's.

VI

It was difficult to advance. Never mind. A few hours later I found myself high up on the fjeld; I must have strayed from the path. What is that dark shape there? A mountain peak. And that over there? Another peak. Let us pitch camp on the spot, then.

There was a deep goodness and tenderness about this mild night. I sat in the dark recalling forgotten memories of my childhood, and many experiences in this place and that. And what a satisfaction it is, too, to have money in one's pocket, even if one sleeps in the open!

During the night I woke up; I found it growing too warm for me under my crag, and loosened my sleeping bag. It seemed to me, too, that a sound still hummed in my ear, as though I had called out or sung in my sleep. Suddenly I felt completely rested, and turned to look about me. It was dark and mild, a stone-still world. The sky was paler than the ring of mountains round me; I lay in the center of a city of peaks, at the foot of a great cliff, huge to the point of deformity. The wind began to blow, and suddenly there was a booming in the distance. Then came a streak of lightning, and immediately after the thunder rolled down like a gigantic avalanche between the most distant peaks. It was matchless to lie there listening, and a supernatural delight, a thrill of enjoyment, ran through me. A stranger madness filled me than I had ever felt before, and I gave it expression by laughing aloud in wanton and humorous abandon. Many a thought ran through my mind, witticisms alternating with moments of such great sorrow that I lay sighing deeply. The lightning and thunder came closer, and it began to rain—a torrential rain. The echoes were overpowering; all nature was an uproar, a hullabalooing. I tried to conquer the night by shouting at it, lest mysteriously it should rob me of my strength and leave me without a will. These mountains, I thought, are sheer incantations against my journey, great planted curses that block my path. Or perhaps I have only strayed into a mountains' trade union? But I nod my head repeatedly. That means I am brave and happy. Perhaps after all they are only stuffed mountains.

More lightning and thunder and torrential rain; it felt as though the near-by echo had slapped me, reverberating a hundred times through me. Never mind. I have read about many battles and been in a rain of bullets before this. Yet in a moment of sadness and humility in the presence of the powers about me, I weep and think:

"Who am I now among men? Or am I lost already? Am I nothing already?"

And I cry out and call my name to hear if it still lives.

A wheel of gold turned before my eyes, and the thunder clapped over my very head, on my own fjeld. Instantly I started out of the sleeping bag and left my shelter. The thunder rolled on, there was lightning and more thunder, worlds were uprooted. Why had I not listened to Olga's advice and remained in the hut? Is it the Lapps whose magic powers are doing this? The Lapps? Those human mites, those mountain dwarfs! What is all this noise to me? I made a feeble effort to walk against it, but stopped again, for I was among giants, and saw the foolishness of trying to battle with the thunder.

I leaned against the side of the mountain: no longer did I stand shouting and hurling challenges at my opponent, but looked at him with milk-blue eyes. And now that I have yielded, none but a mountain would be so hard. But I am not rhymes and rhythms alone; did you think I should waste my good brain chasing such rainbows? You lie. Here I lean against the whole world, and you, perhaps, believe the blue of my eyes....

At that, the lightning struck me. This was a miracle, and it happened to me. It ran down my left elbow, scorching the sleeve of my jacket. The lightning seemed like a ball of wool that dropped to the ground. I felt a sensation of heat, and saw that the ground farther down the mountain was struck a loud blow and then split. A great oppression held me down; a spear of darkness shot through me. And then it thundered beyond all measure, not long and rumbling, but firm and clear and rattling.

The storm passed on.

VII

Next day I arrived at the deserted hut, drenched to the skin, struck by lightning, but in a strangely gentle and yielding mood, as after a punishment. My good fortune in the midst of my ill-luck made me overfriendly to everything; I tramped on without hurting the ground, and I avoided sinful thoughts, though it was spring. I was not even out of temper when I had to retrace my steps across the fjeld to find my way again to the hut. I had time; there was no hurry. I was the first tourist of the spring season, and far too early.

So I remained at my ease in the hut for a few days. Sometimes at night verses and small poems blossomed in my mind as though I had become a real poet. At any rate there were signs that great changes had taken place within me since the winter, when I had desired nothing but to lie blinking my eyes and be left in peace.

One day when everything was thawing in the sun, I left the hut and walked about the mountains for some hours. I had lately been thinking of writing some children's verses, addressed to a certain little girl, but nothing had come of it. Now as I walked on the mountainside, I felt again a desire for this pastime, and worked at it on several occasions, but could not get it into shape. The night, when one has slept an hour or two, is the time when such things come to one.

So I went straight on to the village and bought myself a good store of food. There were many people in this district, and it did me good to hear human speech and laughter again; but there was no place here where I could stay, and in any case I had come too early. I had much to carry on my way home to my hut again. About halfway I met a man, a casual laborer, a vagabond, whose name was Solem. Later I heard that he was the bastard son of a telegraph operator who had been in Rosenlund nearly a generation before.

That this man should have stepped off the path to let me pass with my burden was a good trait in him, and I thanked him and said, "I shouldn't have run over you in any case, ha, ha!"

He asked me if there was much snow on the way to the village. I told him it was much the same as here. "I see," he said, and turned away. I thought that perhaps he had come a long way, and since he carried nothing that looked like provisions, I offered him some of mine in order to make him talk a little. He thanked me and accepted.

He was above middle height, and quite young, not more than in his twenties, possibly just on thirty—a fine fellow. After the swaggering fashion of wanderers, he had a lock of hair escaping from under the peak of his cap; but he wore no beard. This full-grown man still shaved without growing tired of doing so, and this, together with his fringe of hair and his general manner, gave me the impression that he wished to seem younger than he was.

We talked while he ate; he laughed readily and was in a cheerful mood, and since his face was beardless and hard, it looked like a laughing iron mask. But he was sensible and pleasant. There was only one thing: I had been silent for so long that I talked now perhaps too readily; and if it happened that both this boy Solem and I spoke at once, he would stop immediately to let me have my say. When this had happened several times, I grew tired of winning, and stopped too. But that merely made him nod and say: "Go ahead."

I explained to him that I idled in solitude, studying strange trees, and writing a thing or two about them, that I lived in a hut, but that today I had finished my stock of provisions and had had to go to the village. When he heard about the hut, he stopped chewing, and sat as though he were listening; then he said hastily: "Yes, in a way I know these telegraph poles across the mountains very well. Not these particular poles, but others. I was a linesman till not long ago."

"Were you?" I said. "Haven't you passed my hut today?" I added.

He hesitated a moment, but when he saw that I was not trying to put him in the wrong, he admitted that he had been in the hut and rested, and found my crisp-bread there.

"It wasn't easy to sit there without taking some of it," he said.

We spoke of many things. His language was hardly coarse at all, nor did he dawdle over his food. My own manners had run wild to such an extent that I valued his good behavior.

He offered to help me carry my pack as a mark of his gratitude for the food, and I accepted his offer. It was in this way that the stranger returned to the hut with me. As soon as I came in I saw a note on the table, a sort of thanks for the bread; it was an extremely ill-mannered epistle, full of obscene expressions. When Solem saw what I was reading, his iron face broke into a smile. I pretended not to understand the note and threw it back on the table; he picked it up and tore it to shreds.

"I'm sorry you've seen it," he said. "We linesmen have a way of doing that sort of thing, and I'd forgotten I'd left it here."

Soon after this he went out.

He stayed that night and next day, and found a means of repaying me by washing some of my clothes and making himself useful in other ways. There was a large tub outside the hut—had been since the Lapps lived there—which was cracked and leaked abundantly, but Solem stopped the cracks with bacon fat and boiled my clothes in it. It was very funny to watch him imperturbably skimming off the fat that floated up.

He seemed to want to stay till we had finished the provisions again, and then to go with me to the village; but when he heard I was going the other way, to the mountain farm somewhere under the great peaks of the Tore, where summer visitors stayed and many travelers passed, he wanted to go there, too. He was a bird of passage.

"Can't I come with you and help you carry?" he asked me. "I'm used to farm work, too, and perhaps I can get a job there."

VIII

The bustle of spring season had already started at the great farm; men and animals were awake, the barn re-echoed with lowing the whole day long, and the goats had long since been let out to pasture.

It was a long way between neighbors here; one or two cotters had cleared an area in the forest, which they had then bought; apart from that, all the land in sight belonged to the farm. Many new houses had been built here as the traffic over the fjelds increased, and gargoyles, homelike and Norwegian, sat on the gable ends, while the sound of a piano came from the living-room. Do you know the place? You have been here, and the people of the farm have asked after you.

Good days, nothing but good days: a suitable transition from solitude. I speak to the young people who own the homestead now, and to the husband's old father and young sister Josephine. The old man leaves his room to look at me. He is terrifyingly old, perhaps ninety; his eyes are worn and half-crazed, and his figure has shrunk to nothing. He toils with both hands to drag himself into the day, and each time it is as though he left his mother's womb anew and found a world before him:

"Look, how strange, there are houses on the farm," he thinks as he gazes at them. And when the barn doors stand open, he looks at them, too, and thinks:

"Just like a doorway; what can it be? Looks exactly like a doorway...."

And he stands still a long time staring at it.

But Josephine, the daughter of his latest marriage, is young and plays the piano for me. Ah, Josephine! As she runs through the garden, her feet are like a breeze under her skirt. How kind she is to the visitors! Surely she has seen us coming a long way off, Solem and myself, and sat down to play the piano. She has gray, pathetic, young girl's hands—hands which confirm an old observation of mine that one's hands reveal one's sexual character, showing chastity, indifference, or passion.

It is pleasant to watch Josephine crouch down to milk the goat. But

24

she is only doing this now to charm and please the stranger. Ordinarily she has no time for such work, for she is too busy at her indoor tasks, waiting at table and watering the flowers and chatting with me about who climbed the Tore Peak last summer, and who did it the summer before that. These are Josephine's tasks.

Refreshed and rejuvenated, I idle about, stand for a while watching Solem, who has been put to carting manure, then drift on down through the wood to the cotters' houses. Neat, compact houses, barns with room for two cows and a couple of goats in each, half-naked children playing homemade games outside the barns, quarrels and laughter and tears. The men at both places cart manure on sleighs, seeking a path where the snow and ice still lie on the ground, and doing very well with it. I do not descend to the houses, but watch the work from my point of vantage. Well do I know the life of labor, and well do I like it.

It was no small area these cotters had broken up; the homesteads were tiny but the fences surrounding the land included a good section of forest. When the ground was cleared all the way to the fence, this would be a farm with five cows and a horse. Good luck!

The days pass, the windowpanes have thawed, the snow is melting away, green things grow against south walls, and the leaves break out in the woods. My original intention to make great irons hot within me is unchanged; but if I ever thought this an easy task I must be an incredible fool. I do not even know with any certainty if there are irons in me still, or whether I can shape them if there are. Since the winter, life has made me lonely and small; I idle and loiter here, remembering that once things were different. Now that I have reached daylight and men again, I begin to understand all this. I was a different person once. The wave has its feathered crest, and so had I; wine has its fire, and so had I. Neurasthenia, the ape of all the diseases, pursues me.

What then? No, I do not mourn this. Mourn? It is for women to mourn. Life is only a loan, and I am grateful for the loan. At times I have had gold and silver and copper and iron and other small metals; it was a great delight to live in the world, much greater than an endless life away from the world; but pleasure cannot last. I know of no one who has not been through the same thing; but I know of no one who will admit it. How they have declined! But they themselves have said:

"See how everything is better!"

25

At their first jubilee, they left life behind and began a vegetating existence; once one is fifty, the seventies begin. And the irons were no longer red-hot; there were no irons. But by heaven, how stubbornly Simplicity insisted the irons were there, insisted that they were red.

"See the irons!" Simplicity said. "See how red they are!"

As though it mattered that death can be kept off for another twenty years from one who has already begun to perish! I have no use for such a way of thinking; but you have, no doubt, you with your cheerful mediocrity and school education. A one-armed man can still walk; a one-legged man can lie down. Has the forest taught you nothing, then? What have I learned in the forest? That young trees grow there.

In my footsteps walks youth, youth that is shamelessly, barbarously scorned, merely because it is young, scorned by stupidity and degeneration. I have seen this for many years. I know nothing more despicable than your school education and your school-education standards. Whether you have a catechism or a compass by which to guide your life is all the same; come here, my friend, and I will give you a compass made of my latest iron.

IX

A tourist arrived at the farm: the first tourist. And the master of the house himself went with him across the fjeld, and as for Solem, why, he, too, went with him so that he might know the way for later tourists. We found the fat, short, and thin-haired stranger standing in the yard, an elderly, well-to-do man who walked for the sake of his health and the last twenty years of his life. Josephine, the dear girl, made her feet a breeze beneath her skirts, and got him into the living room, with its piano and its earthenware bowls with beaded edges. When he was leaving, he brought out his small change, which Josephine received in her gray, young-girl's fingers. On the other side of the fjeld, Solem was given two crowns for acting as guide, and that was good pay. All went so well that the master himself was content.

"Now they'll be coming," he said. "If only they would leave us in peace," he added.

By this he meant he regretted the good, carefree days that he and his household had enjoyed till now; but in a few weeks a motor road would be opened in the neighboring valley, and then it was a question whether the tourist traffic might not be deflected there. His wife and Josephine were a little afraid it would be; but he himself had held as long as possible to the opinion that all their regular visitors who had come again year after year would remain faithful. No matter how many roads and motor cars they might have in other places, they could not get the peaks of the Tore range anywhere but here.

The master of the house had felt so confident that once more he had much timber lying by the wall of the barn, ready to be built into new cottages, with six new guestrooms, a great hall with reindeer horns and log chairs, and a bathroom. But what was the matter with him today; was he beginning to doubt? "If only they would leave us in peace," he said.

A week later Mrs. Brede arrived with her children; she had a cottage to herself, as in previous summers. So she must be rich and fashionable, this Mrs. Brede, since she had a cottage to herself. She was a charming lady, and her little daughters were well-grown, handsome children. They curtsied to me, making me feel, I don't know why, as though they were giving me flowers. A strange feeling.

Then came Miss Torsen and Mrs. Molie, who were both to stay for the summer. They were followed by Schoolmaster Staur, who would stay a week. Later came two schoolmistresses, the Misses Johnsen and Palm, and still later Associate Schoolmaster Höy and several others—tradesmen, telephone operators, a few people from Bergen, one or two Danes. There were many of us at table now, and the talk was lively. When Schoolmaster Staur was asked if he wanted more soup, he replied: "No, thank you; I require no more!" and then rolled his eyes at us to show that this was the correct thing to say. Between meals we made up small parties, going this way and that on the sides of the fjeld and in the woods. But of transient guests there were few or none at all, and it was really on these that the house would earn well—on rooms for a night, on single meals, on cups of coffee. Josephine seemed to be worrying lately, and her young fingers grew more greedy as they counted silver coins.

Lean brook trout, goat's-meat stew, and tinned foods. Some of the guests were dissatisfied people who spoke of leaving; others praised both the food and the wild mountain scenery. Schoolmistress Torsen wanted to leave. She was tall and handsome and wore a red hat on her dark hair; but there were no suitable young men here, and in the long run it was a bore to waste her holidays so completely. Tradesman Batt, who had been in both Africa and America, was the only possibility, for even the Bergensians amounted to nothing.

"Where's Miss Torsen?" Batt would ask us.

"Here I am; I'm coming," the lady answered.

They did not care for walks up the fjeld, but preferred to go to the woods together, where they talked for hours. But Tradesman Batt did not amount to much either; he was short and freckled, and talked of nothing but money and trade. Besides, he had only a small shop in the town, and dealt in tobacco and fruit. No, he did not amount to much.

One day, during a long spell of rain, I sat talking with Miss Torsen. She was an extraordinary girl, ordinarily proud and reserved, but sometimes talkative, lively, and perhaps a little inconsiderate, too. We sat in the living room, with people coming and going continually, but she did not let that disturb her, and talked in high, clear tones; in her eagerness she sometimes clasped her hands, and then dragged them apart again. After we had been sitting there for some time, Tradesman Batt came in, listened to her for a moment, and then said:

"I'm going out now, Miss Torsen; are you coming?"

She swept him once with her eyes from head to foot; then she turned away and went on talking, looking very proud and determined as she did so. No doubt she had many good qualities; she was twenty-seven, she said, and sick and tired of a teacher's life.

But why had she ever entered on such a life in the first place?

"Oh, just doing what everybody else did," she replied. "The girls next door were also going to walk the road of scholarship; to study languages, as they called it, study grammar; it all sounded so fine. We were going to be independent and earn a lot of money. That's what I thought! Have a home, however small, that was quite my own. How we slogged away all through school! Some of the girls had

28

money, but those of us who were poor couldn't dress like them, and we hadn't well-kept hands like theirs. And so we came to avoid all work at home for the sake of our hands.

"And we played up to the boys at school, too. We thought them such fine gentlemen; one of them had a riding horse, bit of a fool, of course, but he was a millionaire's son and awfully decent, gave us banknotes—me, anyhow—and he kissed me many times. His name was Flaten; his father was a merchant. Of course, he being so handsome and dashing, we wanted to be nice to him too. I should have done anything he asked; I used to pray to God for him.

"I'm sure I wasn't the only one who wanted to be smart and pretty. That was how we passed the time. Washing and cooking and mending fell to the lot of my mother and sisters; we students wouldn't do anything but sit round being very learned and getting seraphic hands. We were quite mad, as I don't mind admitting. It was in the course of those years that we acquired all the distorted ideas we've been burdened with since; we grew dull with school wisdom, anaemic, unbalanced: sometimes terribly unhappy about our sad lot, sometimes hysterically happy, and pluming ourselves on our examinations and our importance. We were the pride of the family.

"And of course we were independent. We got jobs in offices, at forty kroner a month. Because now there was no longer anything in the least extraordinary about us students—we were no rarity, there were hundreds of us—forty kroner was the most they gave us. Thirty went to Father and Mother for our keep, and ten for ourselves. It wasn't enough. We had to have pretty clothes for the office, and we were young, we liked to walk out; but everything was too dear for us, we went into debt, and some of us got engaged to poor devils like ourselves. The narrow school life during our years of development did more than hurt our intelligence; we wanted to show spirit, too, and not recoil before any experience, so some of us went to the bad, others married—and with such antecedents, of course, there was first-rate mismanagement in the home; others disappeared to America. But probably all of them are still boasting their languages and their examinations. It's all they have left—not happiness or health or innocence, but their matriculation. Good God!"

"But surely some of you have become schoolmistresses with good salaries?"

"Good salaries! Anyhow, first we had to start studying all over again.

As though Father and Mother and brothers and sisters hadn't sacrificed enough for our sakes already! There was cramming again for long periods, and then we began life in the schoolroom—to give to others the same unnatural upbringing we had had ourselves. Oh, yes, ours was a noble vocation; it was almost like being missionaries. But now if you'll excuse me, I'd like to talk about something besides this exalted position. Anything else you please."

Tradesman Batt opened the door and said:

"Are you coming, Miss Torsen? It's stopped raining now."

"Oh, leave me alone," she replied.

Tradesman Batt withdrew.

"Why do you turn him away like that?" I asked.

"Because ... well, the weather is bad," she said, looking out of the window. "Besides, he's such a fool. And he takes such liberties."

How sure of herself she looked, and how right she seemed!

Poor Miss Torsen! True or not, the news gradually spread that Miss Torsen had recently lost her post at the school, where indulgence had been exercised for a long time toward her eccentric methods of teaching.

So that was it.

But certainly what she had told me was nonetheless true.

X

The news has leaked out that the master of the homestead here owes a huge debt, and that because he needs cash he has sold new, valuable plots of land to his cotters. I am finding out many things now. Mrs. Brede with the handsome, well-modeled head knows something about everything, for her many summers at the farm have given her knowledge. When she talks about conditions here, she need not grope for words.

The master has taken a large mortgage.

No one would believe that all is not well here; the many new buildings and flagpoles, the curtains at the windows and the red-painted well house—all give an impression of great prosperity. The rooms, too, make a good impression. I shall not speak of the piano, but here are pictures on the walls and photographs of the farm seen from all angles; good newspapers are kept and there is a selection of novels on the tables; though guests sometimes take books away with them, the books are never missed. Or take a thing like this: you get your bill on a handsomely printed paper, with a picture at the top of the farm and the Tore range in the background. In short, no one would doubt for a moment that there is a fortune here. And why not, after twenty years as a kind of resort for tourists and pensioners?

Nevertheless, the truth is that this homestead with all its interior and exterior furnishings costs more than the business is worth. Manufacturer Brede, too, has put money into it, and that is why Mrs. Brede comes here every year with her children, to get their dividends in board and lodging.

No wonder she has a house to herself; after all, it's her own house.

"It was a good place in the old days," says Mrs. Brede. "Travelers stopped here and had a meal and a bed for the night; it cost nothing to run the place then. But the tourist traffic has forced him to make improvements and enlargements. You have to keep pace with development, and be as good as other such places in the country; they're all competing. And probably the master here is not the right man to carry on such an irregular and capricious business; he has learned to like idleness too much, and lets the farm take care of itself. But the two cotters are hard-working fellows. They're nephews of his, and bit by bit they're buying the farm from him and cultivating it. My husband often says it will end with the cotters or their children buying this whole place of his, Paul's."

"How can the cotters get power to do that?"

"They work hard; they're peasants. They started in the forest with three or four goats each, first one of them, then the other one, working down in the village and coming home with food and money, and all the time clearing their own ground. The goats grew more numerous, a cow was added, they bought more virgin land, and they acquired still more livestock. They sowed grain and planted potatoes and cultivated pasture land; the owner here buys root vegetables from his cotters; he hasn't time to toil with such things himself; there's a great deal of work in it. Oh, no, they don't sow anything but green fodder for the stock here; Paul says it's not worth-while. And in a way he's right. He's tried hiring enough men to run the farm too, but it won't work. It's just in the spring season that the tourists start coming, and then the men are constantly being interrupted in their work on the farm to pilot tourists across the fjeld, or to do this or that for the guests. And this goes on all through the short summer months; for several years, they haven't even found the time to spread all their manure. But the worst time is really the autumn, when the tourists are all rushing to get home again, and it's quite impossible to do the harvesting undisturbed. It's almost become a custom here now, my husband says, for the cotters to get half the harvest of the farm's outlying fields."

On my wondering at Mrs. Brede's knowledge of farming, she told me with a shake of the head that she herself knew very little about it, and had all her information from her husband. The fact was that every time these cotters wanted to buy a fresh piece of land from Paul, her husband had to give his consent. This was because of the mortgage, and this, too, was how they had learned of these matters. Manufacturer Brede, as a matter of fact, was most anxious to be released from his undertaking, but this was by no means easy. It was with great apprehensions that he now regarded the new automobile route.

Mrs. Brede was full of a maternal gentleness; she played with her little girls, and seemed to enjoy an admirable balance of mind. One day, for example, a goat came home with one of its hind legs broken, and all the guests hurried out with brandy and lanolin and bandages for the wound; but Mrs. Brede remained quietly where she was, experienced, wise, and a little surprised at all the excitement.

"All you can do with such a goat," she said, "is to slaughter it."

The lady, I understood, must have married early, for her two little girls were twelve and ten. Her husband seemed to deal in important business, for he spent a large part of the year in Iceland, and traveled a good deal elsewhere as well. This, too, the lady bore quietly. And yet she was still young and handsome, a little plump, perhaps, for her height, but with a lovely, unwrinkled skin. She was quite unlike Miss Torsen, the only other good-looking lady at the farm; Miss Torsen was tall and dark.

But perhaps Mrs. Brede was not always so calm as she seemed. One evening when she went down to the men's hut and asked Solem to do her a service, I saw that her face was strange and covered with blushes. Would Solem come to her room and repair a window-blind that had fallen down? It was late in the evening, and the lady seemed to have been in bed already, and to have risen again. Solem did not appear very willing. Suddenly their eyes met, and clung for a moment. Yes, certainly, of course he would come....

What an iron face he had, and what a rogue he was!

Mrs. Brede departed.

But a moment later she returned to say that she had changed her mind. Never mind, thank you, she would fix the blind in position herself.

XI

An occasional tourist came or went, Solem accompanied him across the fjeld, and he was gone. But where were all the foreigners this year? Bennett's and Cook's conducted tours, the hordes that would "do" the mountain peaks of Norway—where were they?

At last two solitary Englishmen turned up. They were middle-aged, unshaven and ill-groomed altogether, two engineers or something of that sort, but quite as speechless and uncivil as the grandest of the traveling British clowns. "Guide! Guide!" they called. "You the guide?" Nothing about them was any different from what we had grown to expect; these two traveled brainlessly and solemnly to the mountain tops, were in a hurry, had a purpose, behaved as though they were running to catch a doctor. Solem went with them to the top and down the other side, and they offered him a fifty-öre bit. Solem held out the palm of his hand, he told me afterwards, for he thought they would put more in it, but nothing came of that. So he created a disturbance—Solem has grown spoiled and insolent from all his idling with tourists.

"Mehr, more," said he.

No, they would not. Solem flung the coin on the ground and struck his hands together repeatedly. This had the required effect, and one krone made its appearance. But on Solem's taking the noble lord by the shoulder and exerting a little pressure, two kroner were at last forthcoming.

At length a conducted party arrived. Many tongues, both sexes, huntsmen, fishermen, dogs, mountaineers, porters. There was a tremendous commotion at the farm; the flag was run up, Paul bent double under all the orders he received, and Josephine ran, flew at every call. Mrs. Brede had to give up her sitting room to three English ladies, and the rest of us were crowded together as close as possible. I, for my part, was to be allowed to keep my bed because of my settled age; but I said, "By no means, let this English solicitor or whatever he is have my bed; what does it matter for a night!"

Then I went out.

If one keeps one's eyes open, one may see a great deal at such a resort in the daytime. And one may see much at night, too. What is the meaning of all this bleating of goats in the shed? Why are the animals not at rest? The door is closed; none of the visiting dogs has got in. Or—have some of the visiting dogs got in? Vice, like virtue, walks in rings and circles; nothing is new, all returns to its beginnings and repeats itself. The Romans ruled the world, yes. They were so mighty, the Romans, so invincible, that they could permit themselves a vice or two, they could afford to live at the arena, they had their fun with young boys and animals. Then one day retribution overtook them, their children's children lost battles everywhere, and their children's children again only sat—sat and looked backward. The ring was closed; none were less rulers of the world than the Romans.

They paid no attention to me, the two Englishmen in the goats' shed; I was merely one of the natives, a Norwegian, who had but to accept the ways of the mighty tourists. But they themselves belonged to that nation of gamblers, coachmen, and vice which one day the wholesome Gothic soul will castigate to death....

The disturbance continued all night, and very early, the dogs began to bark. The caravan awoke; it was six in the morning, and doors began to bang in all the houses. They were in a great hurry, these travelers; they were running to catch the doctor. They had breakfast in two sessions, but though the household was bent double before them and gave of its best, they were not satisfied. "If we had only known a little earlier," said Paul. But they muttered that we should

34

just wait; there were motor cars in other places. Then Paul spoke—Paul, the master of the farm, the man who lived under the Tore peaks:

"But I'm going to enlarge; don't you see all the timber outside? And I'm planning to get a telephone...."

The caravan paid the exact amount of their small bill and departed, accompanied by the master and Solem, both carrying trunks.

Peace descended on us again.

Schoolmaster Staur left now, too. He had been busy collecting plants round the Tore peaks, and talked about his plants at table in a very learned fashion, giving the Latin names, and pointing out their peculiarities. Yes, indeed, he had learned a great deal at school.

"Here you see an Artemis cotula," he said.

Miss Torsen, who had also imbibed much learning, recognized the name and said:

"Yes, take plenty of it with you."

"What for?"

"It's insect powder."

Schoolmaster Staur knew nothing of that, and there was a good deal of discussion in which Associate Master Höy had to take a hand.

No, Schoolmaster Staur knew nothing of that. But he could classify plants and learn their names by heart. He enjoyed that. The peasant children in his neighborhood were ignorant of these classes and names, and he could teach them. He enjoyed that so much.

But was the spirit of the soil his friend? The plant that is cut down one year, yet grows again the next—did this miracle make him religious and silent? The stones, and the heather, and the branches of trees, and the grass, and the woods, and the wind, and the great heaven of all the universe—were these his friends?

Artemis cotula....

XII

When I get tired of Associate Master Höy and the ladies....
Sometimes I think of Mrs. Molie. She sits sewing while the Associate
Master gravely keeps her company; they talk about the servants at
home whose only desire is to stay out all night. Mrs. Molie is a thin,
flat-chested lady, but probably she has at one time been less plain;
her bluish teeth look as though they were cold, as though they were
made of ice, but perhaps a few years ago, her full lips and the dark
down at the corners of her mouth seemed to her husband the most
beautiful thing he knew. Her husband—well, he was a seafaring
man, a ship's captain; he only came home on rare occasions, just
often enough to increase the family; usually he was in Australia,
China, or Mexico. It was hail and farewell with him. And here is his
wife now for the sake of her health. I wonder—is it only for her
health, or are she and the Associate Master possibly children of the
same provincial town?

When I get tired of Associate Master Höy and the ladies, I leave
them and go out. And then I stay out all day long and nobody knows
where I keep myself. It is fitting that a settled man should be
different from the Associate Master, who is very far from being so
settled. So I go out. It is a bright day with just the right amount of
warmth, and my summer woods are filled with the fragrance of
plants. I rest frequently, not because I need to, but because the
ground is full of caresses. I go so far that no one can find me; only
then am I released. No sound reaches me from farms or men, no
one is in sight; only this overgrown little goat track, which is green
at the edges and lovely. Only a bit of a goat track which looks as
though it had fallen asleep in the woods, lying there so thin and
lonely.

You who read this feel nothing, but I who sit here writing feel a kind
of sweetness at the memory of a mere track in the woods. It was like
meeting a child.

With my hands under my neck and my nose in the air, my eyes flit
across the sky. High up above the peaks of Tore, a clustering mist
sways in slow rhythm, breaks apart and presses close again,
fluctuates and strains to give birth to something. But when I rise to
walk on, the end is not yet in sight.

I meet a line of ants, a procession of ants, busy travelers. They

36

neither toil nor carry anything; they simply move. I retrace my steps to see if I can find their leader, but it is useless: farther and farther I retreat, I begin to run, but the procession is endless before and behind me. Perhaps they started a week ago. So I go on my way, and the other insects go on theirs.

Surely this is not a mountainside I walk on; this is a bosom, an embrace, in its softness. I tread gently, for I do not wish to stamp or weigh it down, and I marvel: a mountain so tender and defenseless, indulgent like a mother. To think of an ant walking on this! Here and there lie stones, half-covered with moss, not because they have fallen there, but because this is their home, and they have lived here long. This is peerless.

When I reach the top and look back, it is high noon. Far away on another peak walks one of the cows of the cotters, a strange little cow with red and white flanks. A crow sits on a high cliff above me and caws down at me in a voice like an iron rasp scraping against the stone. A warm thrill runs through me, and I feel, as I have done in the woods so many times before, that someone has just been here, and has stepped to one side. Someone is with me here, and a moment later I see his back disappearing into the woods. "It is God," I think. There I stand, neither speaking nor singing. I only see. I feel all my face being filled with the sight. "It was God," I think.

"A vision," you say. "No, a little insight into things," I reply. "Am I making a god of nature? Do not you? Have not the Mohammedans their god, the Jews theirs, the Hindus theirs? No one knows God, my friend; man knows only gods. And sometimes I meet mine."

I go home by a different route, which forms a vast arc with the one I came by. The sun is warmer now and the ground less smooth. I reach a great ruin, the remnant of a landslide, and here, to amuse myself, I pretend to be tired, flinging myself on the ground exactly as though someone were watching me and saw how exhausted I am. It is only for my amusement, because my brain has been idle so long. The sky is clear everywhere; the clusters of mist over the Tore peaks are gone, heaven knows where, but they have stolen away. In their place, an eagle swings in great circles over the valley. Huge, black, and inaccessible, he traces ring after ring as though held on a rail in the air, moving with voluptuous languor, a thick-necked male, a winged stallion exulting. It is like music to watch him. At length he disappears behind the peaks.

And here are only myself and the ruin and the little juniper trees. What miracles all things are! These stones in the ruin perhaps hold some meaning; they have lain here for thousands of years, but perhaps they, too, roam, and make an inexpressible journey. The glaciers move, the land rises, and the land falls; there is no hurry here. But since my consciousness cannot associate fact with such a conception, it grows blind with fury and revolts: The ruin cannot move; these are mere words, a game!

This ruin is a town; here and there lie scattered buildings of stone. It's a peaceable gathering, without sensations or suicides, and perhaps a well-shaped soul sits in each of these stones. But heaven protect me just the same from the inhabitants of these towns! Rolling stones cannot bark, neither do they attract thieves; they are mere ballast. Quiet behavior: that is what I hold against them, that they make no fiery gestures; it would become them to roll a little, but there they lie, with even their sex unknown. But you saw the eagle instead! Be still....

A gentle wind begins to blow, swaying the bracken a little, the flowers and the straw; but the straw cannot sway, it only trembles.

I walk on along my great arc and come down by the first cotter's house.

"Well, I expect you'll end up by building a summer resort too," I tell him in the course of our conversation.

"Oh, no; we couldn't venture on anything like that," he replies cunningly. In his heart I daresay he has no desire to, for he has seen what it leads to.

I didn't like him; his eyes were fawning and rested on the ground. He thought of nothing but land; he was land-greedy, like an animal that sought to escape its padlock. The other cotter had bought a slightly larger piece of land than he, a marsh that would feed one cow more; but he himself had only got this bit of a field. Still, this would amount to something, too, as long as he kept his health to work it.

He gripped his spade again.

XIII

Solem was being discussed at dinner; I don't know who began it, but some of the ladies thought he was good-looking, and they nodded and said, Yes, he was the right sort.

"What do you mean by the right sort?" Associate Master Höy asked, looking up from his plate.

No one answered.

Then Associate Master Höy could not help smiling broadly, and said:

"Well, well! I must have a look at this Solem some time. I've never paid any attention to him."

Associate Master Höy might look at Solem all he pleased; he would grow no bigger for that, nor Solem smaller. The good Mr. Höy was annoyed, and that was the truth. It is catching for a woman to discover that a man is "the right sort"; the other women grow curious, and stick their noses into it: "So-o-o, is he?" And a few days later the whole flock of them are of one opinion: "Yes, indeed, he's the right sort!"

Pity the poor, left-over associate masters then!

Poor Mr. Höy; there was Mrs. Molie, too, nodding her head for Solem. To tell the truth, she had no appearance of knowing much about the matter, but she could not lag behind the others.

"So, Mrs. Molie is nodding, too!" said Mr. Höy, and smiled again. He was intensely annoyed. Mrs. Molie turned pink and pretty.

At the next meal, Mr. Höy could contain himself no longer.

"Ladies," he said, "mine eyes have now beheld Master Solem."

"Well?"

"Common sneak-thief!"

"Oh, shame!"

"You must admit he has a brazen look on his face. No beard. Blue chin, a perfect horse-face...."

"There's no harm in that," said Mrs. Molie.

Mrs. Molie doesn't seem to have gone quite out of circulation after all, I thought. In fact, she had lately been developing quite a little cushion over her chest, and no longer looked so hunched up. She had eaten well and slept well, and improved at this resort. Mrs. Molie, I suspect, still has plenty of life left in her.

This proved true a few days later. Once again: poor Associate Master Höy! For now we had a new visitor at the farm, a gay dog of a lawyer, and he talked more to Mrs. Molie than to anyone else. Had there been anything between her and Mr. Höy? True, he was not much to look at, but then neither was she.

The young lawyer was a sportsman, yet he was learned in the social sciences, too, had been in Switzerland and studied the principle of the referendum. At first he had worked a few years in an architect's office, he told us, but then he had changed to the law instead, which in its turn had led him into social problems. No doubt he was a rich and unselfish man to be able to change his vocation and to travel in this way. "Ah, Switzerland!" he said, and his eyes watered. None of us could understand his fervor.

"Yes, it must be a wonderful country," Mrs. Molie said.

The Associate Master looked ready to burst, and was quite incapable of restraining himself.

Speaking of Solem, he said suddenly, "I've changed my mind about him lately. He's ten times better than many another."

"There, you see!"

"Yes, he is. And he doesn't pretend to be anything more than he is. And what he is, is of some use. I saw him slaughter the lame goat."

"Did you stop to watch that?"

"I happened to be passing. It was the work of a moment for him. And later I saw him in the woodshed. He knows his job, that fellow. I can well understand that the ladies see something in him."

How the Associate Master clowned! He finished by imploring the wife of the captain who was sailing the China seas to be sure and remain faithful to her Chinaman.

"Do be quiet and let the lawyer tell us about Switzerland," said Mrs. Molie.

Witch! Did she want to drive her fellow-being the Associate Master into jumping off the highest peak of the Tore tonight?

But then Mrs. Brede took a hand. She understood Mr. Höy's torment and wanted to help him. Had not this same Mr. Höy just expressed himself kindly about Solem, and was not Solem the lad who one fine evening had caused her to tear down her window blind? There is cause and effect in all things.

"Switzerland," said Mrs. Brede in her gentle fashion, and then she reddened and laughed a little. "I don't know anything about Switzerland; but once I bought some dress material that was Swiss, and I've never in my life been so cheated."

The lawyer only smiled at this.

Schoolmistress Johnsen talked about what she had learned, watchmakers and the Alps and Calvin—

"Yes, those are the only three things in a thousand years," said the Associate Master, his face quite altered and pale with suppressed rage.

"Really, really, Associate Höy!" exclaimed Schoolmistress Palm with a smile.

But the lawyer focused everyone's admiration on himself by telling them all about Switzerland, that wonderful country, that model for all small countries of the world. What social conditions, what a referendum, what planning in the exploitation of the country's natural wonders! There they had sanatoriums; there they knew how to deal with tourists! Tremendous!

"Yes, and what Swiss cheese," said the Associate Master. "It smells like tourists' feet."

Dead silence. So Associate Master Höy was prepared to go to such lengths!

"Well, what about Norwegian old-milk cheese?" said a Danish voice mildly.

"Yes, that's filthy stuff, too," Mr. Höy replied. "Just the thing for Schoolmaster Staur pontificating in his armchair."

Laughter.

Since matters were now smoothed over again, the lawyer could safely continue:

"If we could only make such Swiss cheese here," he said, "we should not be so poor. Generally speaking, I found after my modest investigations in that country that they are ahead of us in every respect. We have everything to learn from them: their frugality, their diligence, their long working hours, the small home industries—"

"And so on," interrupted Associate Master Höy. "All trifles, nothingness, negativity! A country that exists thanks only to the mercy of its neighbors ought not to be a model for any other country on earth. We must try to rise above the wretched stench of it, which only makes us ill. The big countries and big circumstances should be our model. Everything grows, even the small things, unless they're predestined to a Lilliput existence. A child can learn from another child, of course, but the model is the adult. Some day the child will be an adult itself. A pretty state of affairs it would be if an eternal child, a born pygmy, were to be its model! But that's what all this rubbish about Switzerland really amounts to. Why on earth should we, of all people, take the smallest and meanest country as our model? Things are small enough here anyhow. Switzerland is the serf of Europe. Have you ever heard of a young South American country of Norway's size trying to be on a level with Switzerland? Why do you think Sweden is taking such great strides forward now? Not because it looks to Switzerland, or to Norway, but to Germany! Honor to Sweden for that! But what about us? We don't want to be a piddling little nation stuck up in our mountains, a nation that brings forth peace conferences, ski-runners, and an Ibsen once every thousand years; we have potentialities for a thousand times more—"

The lawyer had for some time been holding up his hand to indicate that he wanted to reply; now he shouted at the top of his voice:

"Just a moment!"

The Associate Master stopped.

"Just one question—a small, trifling question," said the lawyer,

42

preparing his ground well. "Have you ever once set foot in the country you speak of?"

"I should think I have," replied the Associate Master.

There! The lawyer got nothing for his trifling question. And then it all came out what a heartless jilt Mrs. Molie was. She had known all the time that Mr. Höy had been on a traveling scholarship in Switzerland, but she had never mentioned it. What a snake in the grass! She had even encouraged the lawyer, but no one else, to talk about Switzerland.

"Oh, yes, of course Associate Master Höy has been in Switzerland" she said, as though to clinch the matter.

"In that case, the Associate Master and I have looked on the country with different eyes; that's all," said the lawyer, suddenly anxious to end the controversy.

"They haven't even folk tales there," said the Associate Master, who seemed unable to stop. "There they sit, generation after generation, filing watch springs and piloting Englishmen up their mountains. But it's a country without folk music or folk tales. I suppose you think we ought to work hard to resemble the Swiss in that, too?"

"What about William Tell?" asked Miss Johnsen.

Several of the ladies nodded, or at any rate Miss Palm did.

At this point Mrs. Molie turned her head and looked out of the window as she said:

"You really had a very different opinion about Switzerland before, Mr. Associate Master."

This was a hit below the belt. He wanted to reply, wanted to annihilate her, but he restrained himself and remained silent.

"Don't you remember?" she asked, goading him.

"No," he replied. "You mistook my meaning. Really, I can't understand it, I usually make myself quite clear; after all, I'm accustomed to explaining to children."

Another foul. Mrs. Molie said no more, merely smiling patiently.

"I can only say that my opinion is diametrically opposed to yours," the lawyer repeated. "But I did think," he went on, "that this was one thing I knew something about, however...."

Mrs. Molie got up and went out with her head bent, seemingly on the point of bursting into tears. The Associate Master sat still for a moment, and then followed her, whistling and putting on as brave a manner as though he felt quite easy in his mind.

"What's your opinion?" asked Mrs. Brede, turning to the doyen of the company, namely myself.

And as becomes a man of settled years, I replied:

"Probably there has been a little exaggeration on both sides."

Everybody agreed with this. But I could never have acted as a mediator, for I thought the Associate Master was right. In one's early seventies, one still has many pathetically young ideas.

The lawyer rounded off the discussion thus:

"Well, when all's said and done we have Switzerland to thank for being able to sit here at our ease in this comfortable mountain resort. We get tourists into the country on the Swiss model, and earn money and pay off our debts. Ask this man if he would have been willing to do without all we have learned from Switzerland...."

That evening Mrs. Brede asked,

"Why did you make Mr. Höy look so unreasonable today, Mrs. Molie?"

"I?" said Mrs., Molie innocently. "Well, really—!"

As a matter of fact, it seemed as though Mrs. Molie had really been innocent, for the very next morning she and the Associate Master set off up the fjeld together in a very gay mood, and remained away till midday. If they had the matter out between them, then no doubt the lady spoke to her much-tried friend as follows:

"Surely you can see I'm not interested in that lawyer-person! What an idea! I only drew him out so you'd have the chance to give him a good dressing down—don't you understand that? Really, you're the silliest, sweetest—come here, let me kiss you...."

XIV

Since the departure of the great caravan, there have been no other visitors. Some of us cannot understand it; others have in a manner of speaking got a whiff of what is wrong; but all of us still believe there will be more visitors, because after all we're the only ones that have the Tore peaks!

But no one appears.

The women of the house do their daily work for the inmates and do not complain, but they are not happy. Paul still takes things quietly; he sleeps a great deal in his room behind the kitchen, but once or twice I have seen him walking away from the house at night, walking in deep thought toward the woods.

From the neighboring valley comes the rumor that the motor traffic has started there now. So this is the explanation of the quiet in our valley! Then one day a Dane came down to us from the fjeld. He had climbed the Tore peaks from the other side, something that had been thought impossible till now. He had simply driven in a car to the foot of the mountains and walked across!

So we no longer had the Tore peaks to ourselves, either.

I wonder whether, after all, Paul is not going to try to sow green-fodder in the long strip of land down by the river. That, at any rate, had been his original intention, but then came the great caravan, and he neglected it. Now, of course, the season is too far advanced for sowing, and there will be nothing but docks and chickweed. Could not the field be turfed, at least, and sown? Why didn't Paul think of such things instead of walking the woods at night?

But Paul has many thoughts. At an early age, his interest in farming was diverted to the tourist traffic, and there it has remained. He hears that our lawyer is also an architect and asks him to draw a plan for the big new house with the six rooms, the hall and the bathroom. Paul has already ordered the log chairs and the reindeer horns for the hall.

"If you weren't alone up here, you might have got some of the cars coming here too," said the lawyer.

"I've thought of that," Paul replied. "It's not impossible I can do something about it. But I must have the house first. And I must have a road."

The lawyer promised to draw a plan of the house, and went round to look at the site. The house was to cost such and such a sum. Paul was already quite convinced that three or four good tourist summers would pay it off.

Paul was not worrying. As we looked over the site together, I discovered that he smelled of brandy.

Finally a small party of Norwegians and foreigners arrived, travelers who were out to walk, and not to drive in cars. Everyone's spirits rose; the strangers stayed a few days and nights, and were guided across the fjeld by Solem, who earned a fair penny. Paul, too, was visibly cheered, and strolled about the farm in his Sunday clothes. He had a few things to discuss with the lawyer about the house.

"If there's anything to consult about, we had better do it now," he said. "I shall be away for a couple of days."

So they attended to a few minor matters.

"Are you going to town?" asked the lawyer.

"No," Paul replied; "only down to the village. I want to see if I can get the people there to co-operate on a few ideas of mine: a telephone and automobile service and so on."

"Good luck!" said the lawyer.

So the lawyer sat drafting plans while the rest of us went about our own affairs. Josephine went to Solem and said:

"Will you go and sow the field by the river?"

"Has Paul said so?" he asked.

"Yes," she replied.

Solem went very unwillingly. While he was drawing the harrow, Josephine went down to him and said:

"Harrow it once more."

What a brisk little thing she was, with far more forethought than the men! She looked bewitching, for all her hard work. I have seen her

46

many times with her hair tumbled, but it didn't matter. And when she pretended that none but the maids milked the goats and did outside work, it was for the good name of the house. She had learned to play the piano for the same reason. The mistress of the house helped her nobly, for both women were thoughtful and industrious, but Josephine was everywhere, for she was light as a feather. And the chaste little hands she had!

"Josephine, Joséfriendly!" I called her wittily.

XV

Our dark beauty, Miss Torsen, was now seriously considering taking her departure. She was healthy enough in any case, so she did not need a stay in the mountains on that account, and if she was bored, why should she stay?

But a minor event caused her to stay.

In their lack of occupation, the ladies at the resort began to cultivate Solem. They ate so much and grew so fat and healthy that they felt a need to busy themselves with something, and to find someone to make a fuss over. And here was the lad Solem. They got into the habit of telling one another what Solem had said and what Solem believed, and they all listened with great interest. Solem himself had grown spoiled, and joked disrespectfully with the ladies; he called himself a great chap, and once he had even bragged in a most improper way, saying:

"Look, here's a sinful devil for you!"

"Do you know what Solem said to me?" asked Miss Palm. "He's chopping wood and he's got a bandage on his finger, and it keeps getting caught in the wood and bothers him, poor fellow. So he said: 'I wish I had time to stop so I could chop this blasted finger right off my hand!'"

"Tough, isn't he?" said the other ladies. "He's quite capable of doing it, too!"

A little later I passed the woodshed and saw Mrs. Brede there, tying

47

a fresh bandage on Solem's finger.... Poor lady! She was chaste, but young.

The days have been oppressively warm for some time now, with the heat coming down in waves from the mountain and robbing us of all our strength. But in the evenings we recovered somewhat, and busied ourselves in various ways: some of us wrote letters or played forfeit games in the garden, while others were so far restored that they went for a walk "to look at nature."

Last Sunday evening I stood talking to Solem outside his room. He had on his Sunday clothes, and seemed to have no intention of going to bed.

Miss Torsen came by, stopped, and said:

"I hear you're going for a walk with Mrs. Brede?"

Solem removed his cap, which left a red ring round his forehead.

"Who, me?" he said. "Well, maybe she said something about it. There was a path through the woods she wanted me to show her, she said."

Miss Torsen was filled with madness now; handsome and desperate, she paced back and forth; you could almost see the sparks flying. Her red felt hat was held on the back of her head by a pin, the brim turned up high in front. Her throat was bare, her frock thin, her shoes light.

It was extraordinary to watch her behavior; she had opened a window onto her secret desires. What cared she for Tradesman Batt! Had she not toiled through her youth and gained school knowledge? But no reality! Poor Miss Torsen. Solem must not show a path to any other lady tonight.

As nothing more was said, and Solem was preparing to depart, Miss Torsen cleared her throat.

"Come with me instead!" she said.

Solem looked round quickly and said, "All right."

So I left them; I whistled as I walked away with exaggerated indifference, as though nothing on earth were any concern of mine.

"Come with me instead," she said. And he went. They were already behind the outhouses, then behind the two great rowan trees; they hurried lest Mrs. Brede should see them. Then they were gone.

A door wide open, but where did it lead? I saw no sweetness in her, nothing but excitement. She had learned grammar, but no language; her soul was undernourished. A true woman would have married; she would have been a man's wife, she would have been a mother, she would have been a benediction to herself. Why pounce on a pleasure merely to prevent others from having it? And she so tall and handsome!

The dog stands growling over a bone. He waits till another dog approaches. Then suddenly he is overcome with gluttony, pounces on the bone and crushes it between his teeth. Because the other dog is approaching.

It seemed as though this small event had to happen before my mind was ready for the night. I awoke in the dark and felt within me the nursery rhyme I had dawdled over so long: four rollicking verses about the juniper tree.

> To the top of the steepest mountains,
> where the little juniper stands,
> no other tree can follow
> from all the forest lands.
> Halfway to the hilltop
> the shivering pine catches hold;
> the birch has actually passed him,
> though sneezing with a cold.
> But a little shrub outstrips them,
> a sturdy fellow he,
> and stands quite close to the summit,
> though he measures barely a yard.
> They look like a train from the valley below
> with the shortest one for the guard.
> Or else perhaps he's a coachman now—
> why, it's only a juniper tree.
>
> Down dale there's summer lightning,
> green leaves and St. John's feast,
> with songs and games of children,
> and a dozen dances at least.
> But high on the empty mountain
> stands a shrub in lonely glory,

with only the trolls that prowl about,
just like in a story.
The wind with the juniper's forelock
is making very free;
it sweeps across the world beneath
that lies there helpless and bare,
but the air on the heights is fresher
than you'll ever find it elsewhere.
None can see so far around
as such a juniper tree.

There hovers over the mountain
for a moment summer's breath;
at once eternal winter
brings back his companion, death.
Yet sturdy stands the juniper
with needles ever green.
I wonder how the little chap
can bear a life so lean.
He's hard as bone and gristle,
as anyone can see;
when every other tree is stripped,
his berries are scarlet and sleek,
and every berry's plainly marked
with a cross upon its cheek.
So now we know what he looks like too,
this jolly juniper tree.

At times I think he sings to himself
a cheerful little song:
"I've got a bright blue heaven
to look at all day long!"
Sometimes to his juniper brothers
he calls that they need not fear
the trolls that are prowling and peering
about them far and near.
Gently the winter evening
falls over the copse on the height,
and a thousand stars and candles
are lit in the plains of the sky.
The juniper trees grow weary
and nod their heads on the sly;
before we know it they're fast asleep,
so we say: "Good night, good night!"

I got up and wrote out these rhymes on a sheet of paper, which I sent to a little girl, a child with whom I had walked much in the country, and she learned them at once. Then I read them to Mrs. Brede's little girls, who stood still like two bluebells, listening. Then they tore the paper out of my hand and ran to their mother with it. They loved their mother very much. And she loved them too; they had the most delightful fun together at bedtime.

Brave Mrs. Brede with her children! She might have committed a madness, but could not find it in her heart to do so. Yet did anyone prize her for that? Who? Her husband?

A man should take his wife to Iceland with him. Or risk the consequences of her being left behind for endless days.

XVI

Miss Torsen no longer talks about leaving. Not that she looks very happy about staying, either; but Miss Torsen is altogether too restless and strange to be contented with anything.

Naturally she caught cold after that evening in the woods with Solem, and stayed in bed with a headache next day; when she got up again, she was quite all right.

Was she? Why was her throat so blue under the chin, as though someone had seized her by it?

She never went near Solem any more, and behaved as though he were nonexistent. Apparently there had been a struggle in the woods that had made her blue under the chin, and they were friends no longer! It was like her to want nothing real, nothing but the sensation, nothing but the triumph. Solem had not understood that, and had flown into a passion. Had it been thus?

Yes, there was no doubt that Solem had been cheated. He was more direct and lacked subtlety; he made allusions, and said things like "Oh, yes, that Miss Torsen, she's a fine one; I'll bet she's as strong as a man!"

And then he laughed, but with repressed fury. He followed her with

51

gross eyes wherever she went, and in order to assert himself and seem indifferent, he would sing a song of the linesman's life whenever she was about. But he might have saved himself the trouble. Miss Torsen was stone-deaf to his songs.

And now it seemed she was going to stay at the resort out of sheer defiance. We enjoyed her company no more than we had done before, but she began to make herself agreeable to the lawyer, sitting by his work table in the living room as he drew plans of houses. Such is the perverse idleness of summer resorts.

So the days pass; they hold no further novelty for me, and I begin to weary of them. Now and then comes a stranger who is going across the fjeld, but things are no longer, I am told, as they were in other years, when visitors came in droves. And things will not improve until we, too, get roads and cars.

I have not troubled to mention it before this, but the neighboring valley is called Stordalen (Great Valley), while ours is only called Reisa after the river: the whole of the Reisa district is no more than an appendage. Stordalen has all the advantages, even the name. But Paul, our host, calls the neighboring valley Little Valley, because, says Paul, the people there are so petty and avaricious.

Poor Paul! He has returned from his tour to the village as hopeless as he went, and hopelessly drunk besides. For more than a day, he stayed in his room without once emerging. When he reappeared at last, he was aloof and reserved, pretending he had been very successful during his absence; he should manage about the cars, never fear! In the evening, after he had had a few more drinks, he became self-important in a different way: oh, those fools in the village had no sense of any kind, and had refused to give their consent to a road to his place. He was the only one with any sense. Would not such a bit of a road be a blessing to the whole appendage? Because then the caravans would come, scattering money over the valley. They understood nothing, those fools!

"But sooner or later there will have to be a road here," said the lawyer.

"Of course," replied Paul with finality.

Then he went to his room and lay down again.

On another day, a small flock of strangers came again; they had

52

toiled up themselves, carrying their luggage in the hot sun, and now they wanted some help. Solem was ready at once, but he could not possibly carry all the bags and knapsacks; Paul was lying down in his room. I had seen Paul again during the night go out to the woods, talking loudly and flinging his arms about as though he had company.

And here were all the strangers.

Paul's wife and Josephine came out of the house and sent Solem across to Einar, the first cotter, to ask if he would come and help them carry. In the meantime the travelers grew impatient and kept looking at their watches, for if they could not cross the Tore fjeld before nightfall, they would have to spend the night outdoors. One of them suggested to the others that perhaps this delay was intentional. The owner of the place probably wanted them to spend the night there; they began to grumble among themselves, and at last they asked:

"Where is the master, the host?"

"He's ill," said Josephine.

Solem returned and said:

"Einar hasn't time to come; he's lifting his potatoes."

A pause.

Then Josephine said:

"I've got to go across the fjeld anyhow—wait a minute!"

She was gone for a moment, then returned, loaded the bags and knapsacks on her little back, and trotted off. The others followed.

I caught up with Josephine and took her burden from her. But I would not allow her to turn back, for this little tour away from the house would do her good. We walked together and talked on the way: she had really no complaints, she said, for she had a tidy sum of money saved up.

When we reached the top of the fjeld, Josephine wanted to turn back. She thought it a waste of time to walk by my side, with nothing to do but walk.

"I thought you had to cross the fjeld anyhow?" I said.

She was too shrewd to deny it outright, for in that case she, the daughter of the old man at the Tore Peak farm, would have been going with the tourists solely to carry their luggage.

"Yes, but there's no hurry. I was to have visited someone, but that can wait till the winter."

We stood arguing about this, and I was so stubborn that I threatened to throw all the luggage down the mountainside, and then she would see!

"Then I'll just take them and carry them myself," replied Josephine, "and then you'll see!"

By this time the others had caught up with us, and before I knew what had happened, one of the strangers had come forward and lifted the burden from my back, taken off his cap with a great deal of ceremony, and told me his own and his companions' names. I must excuse them, I really must forgive them; this was too bad, he had been so unobserving....

I told him I could easily have carried him as well as the bags. It is not strength I lack; but day and night I carry about with me the ape of all the diseases, who is heavy as lead. Ah, well, many another groans under a burden of stupidity, which is little better. We all have our cross to bear....

Then Josephine and I turned homeward again.

Yes, indeed, people treat me with uncontrollable politeness; this is because of my age. People are indulgent toward me when I am troublesome to others, when I am eccentric, when I have a screw loose; people forgive me because my hair is gray. You who live by your compass will say that I am respected for the writing I have been doing all these years. But if that were so, I should have had respect in my young days when I deserved it, not now when I no longer deserve it so well. No one—no one in the world—can be expected to write after fifty nearly so well as before, and only the fools or the self-interested pretend to improve after that age.

Now it is a fact that I have been practicing a most distinctive authorship, better than most; I know that very well. But this is due, not so much to my endeavors, as to the fact that I was born with this ability.

I have made a test of this, and I know it is true. I have thought to myself: "Suppose someone else had said this!" Well, no doubt others have said it sometimes, but that has not hurt me. I have gone even further than this: I have intentionally exposed myself to direct contempt from other literary men, and this has not hurt me either. So I am sure of my ground. On the other hand, my way of life has lent me an inner distinction for which I have a right to demand respect, because it is the fruit of my own endeavors. You cannot make me out a small man without lying. Yet one can endure even such a lie if one has character.

You may quote Carlyle against me—how authors are misjudged!— "Considering what book-writers do in the world, and what the world does with book-writers, I should say it is the most anomalous thing the world at present has to show." You may quote many others as well; they will assert that a great to-do is made over me for my authorship as well as my native ability, and my struggle to hammer this ability into a useful shape. And I say only what is the truth, that most of the fuss is made because I have reached an age in which my years are revered.

And that is what seems to me so wrong; it is a custom which makes it easy to hold down the gifted young in a most hostile and arrogant fashion. Old age should not be honored for its own sake; it does nothing but halt and delay the march of man. The primitive races, indeed, have no respect for old age, and rid themselves unhesitatingly of it and of its defects. A long time ago I deserved honor much more, and valued it; now, in more than one sense, I am a richer man and can afford to do without.

Yet now I have it. If I enter a room, respectful silence falls. "How old he's grown!" everyone present thinks. And they all remain silent so that I may speak memorable words in that room. Amazing nonsense!

The noise should raise the roof when I enter: "Welcome, old fellow and old companion; for pity's sake don't say anything memorable to us—you should have done that when you were better able to. Sit down, old chap, and keep us company. But don't let your old age cast a shadow on us, and don't restrain us; you have had your day— now it's our turn...."

This is honest speech.

In peasant homes they still have the right instinct: the mothers preserve their daughters, the fathers their sons, from the rough, unpleasant labors. A proper mother lets her daughter sew while she herself works among the cattle. And the daughter will do the same with her own daughter. It is her instinct.

XVII

Dear me, these human beings grow duller every day, and I see nothing in them that I have not known before. So I sink to the level of watching Solem's increasing passion for Miss Torsen. But that too is familiar and dull.

Solem, after all the attention the ladies have paid him, has a delusion of greatness; he buys clothes and gilt watch chains for the money he earns, and on Sundays wears a white woolen pullover, though it is very warm; round his neck and over his chest lies a costly silk tie tied in a sailor's knot. No one else is so smart as he, as he well knows; he sings as he crosses the farmyard, and considers no one too good for him now. Josephine objects to his loud singing, but Solem lad has grown so indispensable at the resort that he no longer obeys all orders. He has his own will in many things, and sometimes Paul himself takes a glass in his company.

Miss Torsen appears to have settled down. She is very busy with the lawyer, and makes him explain each and every angle he draws in his plans. Quite right of her, too, for undeniably the lawyer is the right man for her, a wit and a sportsman, well-to-do, rather simple-minded, strong-necked. At first Mrs. Molie seemed unable to reconcile herself to the constant companionship of these two in the living room, and she frequently had some errand that took her there; what was she after, Mrs. Molie, of the ice-blue teeth?

At last the lawyer finished his plans and was able to deliver them. He began to speak again about a certain peak of the Tore range which no one had yet climbed, and was therefore waiting to be conquered by him. Miss Torsen objected to this plan, and as she grew to know him better, begged him most earnestly not to undertake such a mad climb. So he promised with a smile to obey her wishes. They were in such tender agreement, these two!

But the blue peak still haunted the lawyer's mind; he pointed it out to his lady, and smacked his lips, his eyes watering again.

56

"Gracious, it makes me dizzy just to look at it!" she said.

So the lawyer put his arm round her to steady her.

The sight was painful to Solem, whose eyes were continually on the pair. One day as we left the luncheon table, he approached Miss Torsen and said:

"I know another path; would you like to see it tonight?"

The lady was confused and a little embarrassed, and said at length:

"A path? No, thank you."

She turned to the lawyer, and as they walked away together, she said:

"I never heard of such brazenness!"

"What got into him?" said the lawyer.

Solem went away, his teeth gleaming in a sneer.

That evening, Solem repeated the performance. He went up to Miss Torsen again and said:

"What about that path? Shall we go now?"

As soon as she saw him coming, she turned quickly and tried to elude him. But Solem did not hesitate to follow her.

"Now I've just got one thing to say," she said, stopping. "If you're insolent to me again, I'll see that you're driven off the farm...."

But it was not easy to drive Solem off the farm. After all, he was guide and porter to the tourists, and the only permanent laborer on the farm as well. And soon the hay would have to be brought in, and casual laborers would be engaged to work under him. No, Solem could not be driven off. Besides, the other ladies were on his side; the mighty Mrs. Brede alone could save him by a word. She held the Tore Peak resort in the palm of her hand.

Solem was not discharged; but he held himself in check and became a little more civil. He seemed to suffer as much as ever. Once at midday, as he was standing in the woodshed, I saw him make a scratch with the ax across the nail of his thumb.

"What on earth are you doing?" I asked.

"Oh, I'm just marking myself," he replied, laughing gloomily. "When this scratch grows out—"

He stopped.

"What then?"

"Oh, I'll be away from here then," he said.

But I had the impression that he meant to say something different, so I probed further.

"Let me look. Well, it's not a deep scratch; you won't be here long then, will you?"

"Nails grow slowly," he muttered.

Then he strolled away whistling, and I set about chopping wood.

A little later Solem returned across the farmyard with a cackling hen under his arm. He went to the kitchen window and called:

"This the kind of hen you want me to kill?"

"Yes," was the reply.

Solem came back to the woodshed and asked me for the ax, as he wanted to behead a few hens. It was easy to see that he did everything on the farm; he was, hand and brain, indispensable.

He laid the hen on a block and took aim, but it was not easy, for she twisted her head like a snake and would not lie still. She had stopped cackling now.

"I can feel her heart jumping inside her," said Solem.

Suddenly he saw his chance and struck. There lay the head; Solem still held the body, which jerked under his hand. The thing was done so quickly that the two sections of the bird were still one in my eyes; I could not grasp a separation so sudden and unbelievable, and it took my sight a second or two to overtake the event. Bewilderment was in the expression of this detached head, which looked as though it could not believe what had happened, and raised itself a little as if to show there was nothing the least bit wrong. Solem let the body go. It lay still for a moment, then kicked its legs, leaped to the

58

ground and began to hop, the headless body reeling on one wing till it struck the wall and spattered blood in wide arcs before it fell at last.

"I let her go too soon after all," said Solem.

Then he went off to fetch another hen.

XVIII

I return to the mad idea of Solem's being discharged. This would, to be sure, have averted a certain disaster here at the farm: but who would fetch and carry then? Paul? But I've told you he just lounges all day in his room, and has been doing so lately more than ever; the guests never see him except through an unsuccessful maneuver on his part.

One evening he came walking across the lawn. He must, in his disregard of time, have thought the guests had already retired, but we all sat outside in the mild darkness. When Paul saw us, he drew himself up and saluted as he passed; then, calling Solem to him, he said:

"You mustn't cross the field again without letting me know. I was right there in my room, writing. The idea of Josephine carrying luggage!"

Paul strode on. But even yet he felt he had not appeared important enough, so he turned round and asked:

"Why didn't you take one of my cotters with you to act as porter?"

"They wouldn't go," Solem replied. "They were busy lifting potatoes."

"Wouldn't go?"

"That's what Einar said."

Paul thought this over.

"What insolence! They'd better not go too far or I'll drive them off the place."

Then the law awoke in the lawyer's bosom, and he asked:

"Haven't they bought their land?"

"Yes," said Paul. "But I'm the master of this farm. I have a say in things too. I'm not without power up here in Reisa, believe me...."

Then he said sternly to Solem:

"You come to me next time."

Whereupon he stalked off to the woods again.

"He's a bit tight again, our good Paul," said the lawyer.

Nobody replied.

"Can you imagine an innkeeper in Switzerland behaving like that?" the lawyer remarked.

Mrs. Brede said gently:

"What a pity! He never drank before."

And at once the lawyer was charitable again:

"I'll have a good talk with him," he said.

There followed a period in which Paul was sober from morning till night, when Manufacturer Brede paid us a visit. The flag was hoisted, and there was great commotion at the farm; Josephine's feet said whrr under her skirt. The manufacturer arrived with a porter; his wife and children went far down the road to meet him, and the visitors at the resort sallied forth too.

"Good morning!" he greeted us with a great flourish of his hat. He won us all over. He was big and friendly, fat and cheerful, with the broad good cheer that plenty of money gives. He became good friends with us at once.

"How long are you staying, Daddy?" his little girls asked, as they clung to him.

"Three days."

"Is that all!" said his wife.

"Is that all?" he replied, laughing. "That's not such a short time, my dear; three days is a lot for me."

"But not for me and the children," she said.

"Three whole days," he repeated. "I can tell you I've had to do some moving to be able to stay as quiet as this, ha, ha!"

They all went in. The manufacturer had been here before and knew the way to his wife's cottage. He ordered soda water at once.

In the evening, when the children had gone to bed, the manufacturer and his wife joined us in the living room; he had brought whisky with him for the gentlemen, and ordered soda water; for the ladies he had wine. It was quite a little party, the manufacturer playing the host with skill, and we were all well satisfied. When Miss Palm played folk melodies on the piano, this heavy-built man grew quiet and sentimental; but he didn't think only of himself, for suddenly he went out and lowered the flag. Flags should be lowered at sunset, he said. Once or twice he went across to the cottage, too, to see if the children were sleeping well. Generally speaking, he seemed fond of the children. Though he owned factories and hotels and many other things, yet he seemed to take the greatest pride of all in possessing a couple of children.

One of the men from Bergen struck his glass for silence, and began to make a speech.

The Bergensians had all long been very quiet and retiring, but here was a perfect occasion for making speeches. Was not here a man from the great world outside, from the heart of life, who had brought them wine and good cheer and festivity? Strange wares up here in this world of blue mountains ... and so on.

He talked for about five minutes, and became very animated.

The manufacturer told us a little about Iceland—a neutral country that neither the Associate Master nor the lawyer had visited, and therefore could not disagree about. One of the Danes had been there and was able to confirm the justness of the manufacturer's impressions.

But most of the time he told cheerful anecdotes:

"I have a servant, a young lad, who said to me one day, when I was in a bad temper: 'You've become a great hand at swearing in Icelandic!' Ha, ha, ha—he appreciated me: 'a great hand at swearing in Icelandic,' he said!"

Everybody laughed, and his wife asked:

"And what did you say?"

"What did I say? Why, I couldn't say anything, could I, ha, ha, ha!"

Then another man from Bergen took the floor: we must not forget we had the family of a real man of the world with us here—his wife, "this peerless lady, scattering charm and delight about her," and the children, dancing butterflies! And a few minutes later, "Hip, hip, hurrah!" followed by a flourish on the piano.

The manufacturer drank a toast with his wife.

"Well, that's that!" was all he said.

Mrs. Molie sat off in a corner talking in a loud voice with the Dane who had come over the top of the Tore from the wrong end; she seemed purposely to be talking so audibly. The manufacturer's attention was attracted, and he asked for further information about the motor cars in the neighboring valley: how many there were, and how fast they could go. The Dane told him.

"But just imagine coming across the fjeld from the other side!" said Mrs. Molie. "It hasn't been done before."

In response to the manufacturer's questions, the Dane told him about this adventurous journey also.

"Isn't there a blue peak somewhere in the mountains about here?" said Mrs. Molie. "I suppose you'll be going up that next. Where ever will you stop?"

Yes, the Dane felt quite tempted by this peak, but said he believed it was unconquerable.

"I should have climbed that peak long ago if you, Miss Torsen, hadn't forbidden me," said the lawyer.

"You'd never have made it," said Mrs. Molie in an indifferent tone. This was probably her revenge. She turned to the Dane again as though ready to believe him capable of anything.

"I shouldn't want anyone to think of climbing that peak," said Miss Torsen. "It's as bare as a ship's mast."

"What if I tried it, Gerda?" the manufacturer asked his wife with a smile. "After all, I'm an old sailor."

"Nonsense," she said, smiling a little.

"Well, I climbed the mast of a schooner last spring."

"Where?"

"In Iceland."

"What for?"

"I don't know, though—all this mountain climbing—I haven't much use for it," said the manufacturer.

"What did you do it for? What did you climb the mast for?" his wife repeated nervously.

The manufacturer laughed.

"The curiosity of the female sex—!"

"How can you do a thing like that! And what about me and the children if you—"

She broke off. Her husband grew serious and took her hand.

"It was stormy, my dear; the sails were flapping, and it was a question of life and death. But I shouldn't have told you. Well—we'd better say good night now, Gerda."

The manufacturer and his wife got up.

Then the first man from Bergen made another speech.

The manufacturer stayed with us for the promised three days, and then made ready to travel again. His mood never changed; he was contented and entertaining the whole time. Every evening one whisky and soda was brought him—no more. Before their bedtime, his little girls had a wildly hilarious half-hour with him. At night a tremendous snoring could be heard from his cottage. Before his arrival, the little girls had spent a good deal of time with me, but now they no longer knew I existed, so taken up with their father

63

were they. He hung a swing for them between the two rowan trees in the field, taking care to pack plenty of rag under the rope so as not to injure the tree.

He also had a talk with Paul; there were rumors that he was intending to take his money out of the Tore Peak resort. Paul's head was bent now, but he seemed even more hurt that the manufacturer should have paid a visit to the cotters to see how they were getting on.

"So that's where he's gone?" he said. "Well, let him stay there, for all I care!"

The manufacturer cracked jokes to the very end. Of course he was a little depressed by the farewells, too, but he had to keep his family's courage up. His wife stood holding one of his arms with both hands, and the children clung to his other arm.

"I can't salute you," the manufacturer said to us, smiling. "I'm not allowed to say good-bye."

The children rejoiced at this and cried, "No, he can't have his arm back; Mummy, you hold him tight, too!"

"Come, come!" the father said. "I've got to go to Scotland, just a short trip. And when you come home from the mountains, I'll be there, too."

"Scotland? What are you going to Scotland for?" the children asked.

He twisted round and nodded to us.

"These women! All curiosity!" he said.

But none of his family laughed.

He continued to us:

"I was telling my wife a story about a rich man who was curious, too. He shot himself just to find out what comes after death. Ha, ha, ha! That's the height of curiosity, isn't it? Shooting yourself to find out what comes after death!"

But he could not make his family laugh at this tale, either. His wife stood still; her face was beautiful.

"So you're leaving now," was all she said.

Mr. Brede's porter came out with his luggage; he had stayed at the farm for these three days in order to be at hand.

Then the manufacturer walked down through the field, accompanied by his wife and children.

I don't know—this man with his good humor and kindliness and money and everything, fond of his children, all in all to his wife—

Was he really everything to his wife?

The first evening he wasted time on a party, and every night he wasted time in snoring. And so the three days and nights went by....

XIX

It is very pleasant here at harvest time. Scythes are being sharpened in the field, men and women are at work; they go thinly clad and bareheaded, and call to one another and laugh; sometimes they drink from a bucket of whey, then set to work again. There is the familiar fragrance of hay, which penetrates my senses like a song of home, drawing me home, home, though I am not abroad. But perhaps I am abroad after all, far away from the soil where I have my roots.

Why, indeed, do I stay here any longer, at a resort full of schoolmistresses, with a host who has once more said farewell to sobriety? Nothing is happening to me; I do not grow here. The others go out and lie on their backs; I steal off and find relish in myself, and feel poetry within me for the night. The world wants no, poetry; it wants only verses that have not been sung before.

And Norway wants no red-hot irons; only village smiths forge irons now, for the needs of the mob and the honor of the country.

No one came; the stream of tourists went up and down Stordalen and left our little Reisa valley deserted. If only the Northern Railway could have come to Reisa with Cook's and Bennett's tours—then Stordalen in its turn would have lain deserted. Meanwhile, the cotters who are cultivating the soil will probably go on harvesting half the crop of the outlying fields for the rest of time. There is every reason to think so—unless our descendants are more intelligent than we, and refuse to be smitten with the demoralizing effects of the tourist traffic.

Now, my friend, you mustn't believe me; this is the point where you must shake your head. There is a professor scuttling about the country, a born mediocrity with a little school knowledge about history; you had better ask him. He'll give you just as much mediocre information, my friend, as your vision can grasp and your brain endure.

Hardly had Manufacturer Brede left when Paul began to live a most irregular life again. More and more all roads were closed to him; he saw no way out and therefore preferred to make himself blind, which gave him an excuse for not seeing. Seven of our permanent guests now left together: the telephone operators, Tradesman Batt, Schoolmistresses Johnsen and Palm, and two men who were in some sort of business, I don't quite know what. This whole party went across the fjeld to Stordalen to be driven about in cars.

Cases of various kinds of foodstuffs arrived for Paul; they were carried up one evening by a man from the village. He had to make several journeys with the side of his cart let down, and bring the cases over the roughest spots one by one. That was the kind of road it was. Josephine received the consignment, and noticed that one of the cases gave forth the sound of a liquid splashing inside. That had come to the wrong place, she said, and writing another address on it, she told the man to take it back. It was sirup that had come too late, she said; she had got sirup elsewhere in the meantime.

Later in the evening we heard them discussing it in the kitchen; the sirup had not come too late, Paul said angrily.

"And I've told you to clear these newspapers away!" he cried. We heard the sound of paper and glass being swept to the floor.

Well, things were not too easy for Paul; the days went by dull and empty, nor had he any children to give him pleasant thoughts at times. Though he wanted to build still more houses, he could not use half those he had already. There was Mrs. Brede living alone with her children in one of them, and since seven of the guests had left, Miss Torsen was also alone in the south wing. Paul wanted at all costs to build roads and share in the development of the tourist traffic; he even wanted to run a fleet of motor cars. But since he had not the power to do this alone and could get no assistance, nothing was left him but to resign himself. And now to make matters worse Manufacturer Brede had said he would withdraw his money....

Paul's careworn face looked out of the kitchen door. Before going out himself he wanted to make sure there was no one about, but he was disappointed in this, for the lawyer at once greeted him loudly: "Good evening, Paul!" and drew him outside.

They strolled down the field in the dusk.

Assuredly there is little to be gained by "having a good talk" with a man about his drinking; such matters are too vital to be settled by talking. But Paul seems to have admitted that the lawyer was right in all he said, and probably left him with good resolutions.

Paul went down to the village again. He was going to the post office; the money he had from the seven departed guests would be scattered to all quarters of the globe. And yet it was not enough to cover everything—in fact not enough for anything, for interest, repayments, taxes, and repairs. It paid only for a few cases of food from the city. And of course he stopped the case of sirup from going back.

Paul returned blind-drunk because he no longer wished to see. It was the same thing all over again. But his brain seemed in its own way to go on searching for a solution, and one day he asked the lawyer:

"What do you call those square glass jars for keeping small fish in—goldfish?"

"Do you mean an aquarium?"

"That's it," said Paul. "Are they dear?"

"I don't know. Why?"

"I wonder if I could get one."

"What do you want it for?"

"Don't you think it might attract people to the place? Oh, well, perhaps it wouldn't."

And Paul withdrew.

Madder than ever. Some people see flies. Paul saw goldfish.

XX

The lawyer is constantly in Miss Torsen's company; he even swings her in the children's swing, and puts his arm around her to steady her when the swing stops. Solem watches all this from the field where he is working, and begins to sing a ribald song. Certainly these two have so ill-used him that if he is going to sing improper songs in self-defense, this is the time to do it; no one will gainsay that. So he sang his song very loud, and then began to yodel.

But Miss Torsen went on swinging, and the lawyer went on putting his arm round her and stopping her....

It was a Saturday evening. I stood talking to the lawyer in the garden; he didn't like the place, and wanted to leave, but Miss Torsen would not go with him, and going alone was such a bore. He did not conceal that the young woman meant something to him.

Solem approached, and lifted his cap in greeting. Then he looked round quickly and began to talk to the lawyer—politely, as became his position of a servant:

"The Danish gentleman is going to climb the peak tomorrow. I'm to take a rope and go with him."

The lawyer was startled.

"Is he—?"

The blankness of the lawyer's face was a remarkable sight. His small, athletic brain failed him. A moment passed in silence.

"Yes, early tomorrow morning," said Solem. "I thought I'd tell you. Because after all it was your idea first."

"Yes, so it was," said the lawyer. "You're quite right. But now he'll be ahead of me."

Solem knew how to get round that.

"No, I didn't promise to go," he said. "I told him I had to go to the village tomorrow."

"But we can't deceive him. I don't want to do that."

68

"Pity," said Solem. "Everybody says the first one to climb the Blue Peak will be in all the papers."

"He'll take offense," the lawyer murmured, considering the matter.

But Solem urged him on:

"I don't think so. Anyhow, you were the first one to talk about it."

"Everybody here will know, and I'll be prevented," said the lawyer.

"We can go at dawn," said Solem.

In the end they came to an agreement.

"You won't tell anyone?" the lawyer said to me.

The lawyer was missed in the course of the morning; he was not in his room, and not in the garden.

"Perhaps the Danish mountaineer can tell us where he is," I said. But it transpired that the Dane had not even thought of climbing the Blue Peak that day, and knew nothing whatever about the expedition.

This surprised me greatly.

I looked at the clock; it was eleven. I had been watching the peak through my field glasses from the moment I got up, but there was nothing to be seen. It was five hours since the two men had left.

At half-past eleven Solem came running back; he was drenched in sweat and exhausted.

"Come and help us!" he called excitedly to the group of guests.

"What's happened?" somebody asked.

"He fell off."

How tired Solem was and drenched to the skin! But what could we do? Rush up the mountainside and look at the accident too?

"Can't he walk?" somebody asked.

"No, he's dead," said Solem, looking from one to another of us as though to read in our faces whether his message seemed credible.

"He fell off; he didn't want me to help him."

A few more questions and answers. Josephine was already halfway across the field; she was going to the village to telephone for the doctor.

"We shall have to get him down," said the Danish mountaineer.

So he and I improvised a stretcher; Solem was instructed to take brandy and bandages to the site of the accident, and the Bergensians, the Associate Master, Miss Torsen, and Mrs. Molie went with him.

"Did you really say nothing to Solem about climbing the peak today?" I asked the Dane.

"No," he replied. "I never said a word about it. If I had meant to go, I should certainly not have wanted company...."

Later that afternoon we returned with the lawyer on the stretcher. Solem kept explaining all the way home how the accident had happened, what he had said and what the lawyer had said, pointing to objects on the way as though this stone represented the lawyer and that the abyss into which he had plunged.... Solem still carried the rope he had not had a chance to use. Miss Torsen asked no more than anyone else, and made purely conventional comments: "I advised him against it, I begged him not to go...."

But however much we talked, we could not bring the lawyer back to life. Strange—his watch was still going, but he himself was dead. The doctor could do nothing here, and returned to his village.

There followed a depressing evening. Solem went to the village to send a telegram to the lawyer's family, and the rest of us did what we thought decent under the circumstances: we all sat in the living room with books in our hands. Now and again, some reference would be made to the accident: it was a reminder, we said, how small we mortals were! And the Associate Master, who had not the soul of a tourist, greatly feared that this disaster would injure the resort and make things still more difficult for Paul; people would shun a place where they were likely to fall off and be killed.

No, the Associate Master was no tourist, and did not understand the Anglo-Saxon mind.

Paul himself seemed to sense that the accident might benefit him rather than do him harm. He brought out a bottle of brandy to console us on this mournful evening.

And since it was a death to which we owed this attention, one of the men from Bergen made a speech.

XXI

The accident became widely known. Newspapermen came from the city, and Solem had to pilot them up the mountain and show them the spot where it had taken place. If the body had not been removed at once, they would have written about that, too.

Children and ignoramuses might be inclined to think it foolish that Solem should be taken from the work in the fields at harvest time, but must not the business of the tourist resort go before all else?

"Solem, tourists!" someone called to him. And Solem left his work. A flock of reporters surrounded him, asked him questions, made him take them to the mountains, to the river. A phrase was coined at the farm for Solem's absences:

"Solem's with death."

But Solem was by no means with death; on the contrary, he was in the very midst of life, enjoying himself, thriving. Once again he was an important personage, listened to by strangers, doling out information. Nor did his audience now consist of ladies only— indeed, no; this was something new, a change; these were keen, alert gentlemen from the city.

To me, Solem said:

"Funny the accident should have happened just when the scratch on my nail has grown out, isn't it?"

He showed me his thumbnail; there was no mark on it.

The newspaper reporters wrote articles and sent telegrams, not only about the Blue Peak and the dreadful death, but about the locality, and about the Tore Peak resort, that haven for the weary, with its wonderful buildings set like jewels in the mountains. What a surprise to come here: gargoyles, living room, piano, all the latest books, timber outside ready for new jewels in their setting, altogether a magnificent picture of Norway's modern farming.

Yes, indeed, the newspapermen appreciated it. And they did their advertising.

The English arrived.

"Where is Solem?" they asked, and "Where is the Blue Peak?" they asked.

"We ought to get the hay in," said Josephine and the wife at the farm. "There'll be rain, and fifty cartloads are still out!"

That was all very well, but "Where is Solem?" asked the English. So Solem had to go with them. The two casual laborers began to cart away the hay, but then the women had no one to help them rake. Confusion was rife. Everyone rushed wildly hither and thither because there was no one to lead them.

The weather stayed fine overnight; it was patient, slow-moving weather. As soon as the dew dried up, more hay would be brought in, perhaps all the hay. Oh, we should manage all right.

More English appeared; and "Solem—the Blue Peak?" they said. Their perverse, sportsmen's brains tingled and thrilled; they had successfully eluded all the resorts on the way, and arrived here without being caught. There was the Blue Peak, like a mast against the sky! They hurried up so fast that Solem was hardly able to keep pace with them. They would have felt for ever disgraced if they had neglected to stand on this admirable site of a disaster, this most excellent abyss. Some said it would be a lifelong source of regret to them if they did not climb the Blue Peak forthwith; others had no desire but to gloat over the lawyer's death fall, and to shout down the abyss, gaping at the echo, and advancing so far out on the ledge that they stood with their toes on death.

But it's an ill wind that blows good to none, and the resort earned a great deal of money. Paul began to revive again, and the furrows in his face were smoothed out. A man of worth grows strong and active with good fortune; in adversity he is defiant. One who is not defiant in adversity is worth nothing; let him be destroyed! Paul stopped drinking; he even began to take an interest in the harvesting, and worked in the field in Solem's place. If only he had begun when the weather was still slow and patient!

But at least Paul began to tackle things in the right spirit again; he only regretted that he had set aside for the cotters those outlying fields from which they were used to getting half the hay; this year he would have liked to keep it himself. But he had given his word, and there was nothing to be done about it.

Besides, it was raining now. Haymaking had to stop; they could not even stack what had already been gathered. Outside, three cartloads of fodder were going to waste.

Before long the novelty of the Tore Peak resort wore off again. The newspapermen wrote and sent telegrams about other gratifying misfortunes, the death on the Blue Peak having lost its news value. It had been an intoxication; now came the morning after.

The Danish mountaineer quite simply deserted. He strapped on his knapsack and walked across the field like one of the villagers, caring no more for the Blue Peak. The commotion he had witnessed in the last week had taught him a lesson.

And the tourists swarmed on to other places.

> "What harm have I done them," Paul probably
> thought, "that they should be going again? Have I been
> too much in the fields and too little with them? But I
> greeted them humbly and took my man out of the
> harvesting work to help them...."

Then two young men arrived, sprouts off the Norwegian tree, sportsmen to their finger tips, who talked of nothing but sailing, cycling, and football; they were going to be civil engineers—the young Norway. They, too, wanted to see the Blue Peak to the best of their ability; after all, one must keep pace with modern life. But they were so young that when they looked up at the peak, they were afraid. Solem had learned more than one trick in tourist company; craftily he led them on, and then extorted money from them in return for a promise not to expose their foolishness. So all was well; the young sprouts came down the mountain again, bragging and showing off their sportsmanship. One of them brought down a bloodstained rag which he flung on the ground, saying,

"There's what's left of your lawyer that fell off."

"Ha, ha, ha, ha!" laughed the other sprout.

Yes, truly, they had acquired dashing ways among their sporting acquaintances.

It rained for three weeks; then came two fine days, and then rain again for a fortnight. The sun was not to be seen, the sky was invisible, the mountain tops had disappeared; we saw nothing but rain. The roofs at the Tore Peak resort began to leak more and more.

The hay that still lay spread on the ground was black and rotting, and the stacks had gone moldy.

The cotters had got their hay indoors during the patient spell. They had carried it, man, woman, and child, on their backs.

The men from Bergen and Mrs. Brede with her children have left for home. The little girls curtsied and thanked me for taking them walking in the hills and telling them stories. The house is empty now. Associate Master Höy and Mrs. Molie were the last to go; they left last week, traveling separately, though both were going to the same small town.

He went by way of the village—a very roundabout route—while she crossed the field. It is very quiet now, but Miss Torsen is still here.

Why do I not leave? Don't know. Why ask? I'm here. Have you ever heard anyone ask: "How much is a northern light?" Hold your tongue.

Where should I go if I did leave? Do you imagine I want to go to the town again? Or do you think I'm longing for my old hut and the winter, and Madame? I'm not longing for any specific place; I am simply longing.

Of course I ought to be old enough to understand what all sensible Norwegians know, that our country is once more on the right road. The papers are all writing about the splendid progress the tourist traffic has made in Stordalen since the motor road was opened— ought I not to go there and feel gratified?

From old habit, I still take an interest in the few of us who are left; Miss Torsen is still here.

74

Miss Torsen—what more is there to be said about her? Well, she does not leave; she stays here to complete the picture of the woman Torsen, child of the middle class who has read schoolbooks all through her formative years, who has learned all about Artemis cotula, but undernourished her soul. That is what she is doing here.

I remember a few weeks ago, when we were infested with Englishmen, a young sprout coming down from the mountain top with a bloodstained rag which he threw on the ground, saying, "Here's what's left of your lawyer that fell off!" Miss Torsen heard it, and never moved a muscle. No, she never mourned the death of the lawyer very keenly; on the contrary, she wrote off at once to ask another friend to come. When he came, he turned out to be a swaggering scatterbrain—a "free lance," he called himself in the visitors' book. I have not mentioned him before because he was less important than she; less important, in fact, than any of us. He was beardless and wore his collar open; heaven knows if he wasn't employed at a theater or in the films. Miss Torsen went to meet him when he came, and said, "Welcome to our mountains," and "Thanks for coming." So evidently she had sent for him. But why did she not leave? Why did she seem to strike root in the place, and even ask others to come here? Yet she had been the first to want to leave last summer! There was something behind this.

XXII

I muse on all this, and understand that her staying here is somehow connected with her carnal desires, with the fact that Solem is still here. How muddled it all is, and how this handsome girl has been spoiled! I saw her not long ago, tall and proud, upright, untouched, walking intentionally close to Solem, yet not replying to his greeting. Did she suspect him of complicity in the death of the lawyer and avoid him for that reason? Not in the least; she avoided him less than before, even letting him take her letters to the post office, which she had not done previously. But she was unbalanced, a poor thing that had lost her bearings. Whenever she could, she secretly defiled herself with pitch, with dung; she sniffed at foulness and was not repelled.

One day, when Solem swore a needlessly strong oath at a horse that was restless, she looked at him, shivered, and went a deep red. But she mastered herself at once, and asked Josephine:

"Isn't that man leaving soon?"

"Yes," Josephine replied, "in a few days."

Though she had seized this opportunity to ask her question with a great show of indifference, I am certain it was an important one to her. She went away in silence.

Yes, Miss Torsen stayed, for she was sexually bound to Solem. Solem's despair, Solem's rough passion that she herself had inflamed, his brutality, his masculinity, his greedy hands, his looks—she sniffed at all this and was excited by it. She had grown so unnatural that her sexual needs were satisfied by keeping this man at a distance. The Torsen type no doubt lies in her solitary bed at night, reveling in the sensation that in another house a man lies writhing for her.

But her friend, the actor? He was in no sense the other's equal. There was nothing of the bull in him, nothing of action, only the braggadocio of the theater....

Here am I, growing small and petty with this life. I question Solem about the accident. We are alone together in the woodshed.

Why had he lied and said the Dane wanted to climb the Blue Peak that unfortunate Sunday morning?

Solem looked at me, pretending not to understand.

I repeated my question.

Solem denied he had said any such thing.

"I heard you," I said.

"No, you didn't," he said.

A pause.

Suddenly he dropped to the floor of the shed, convulsed, without shape, an outline merely; a few minutes passed before he got up again. When he was on his feet once more, pulling his clothes to rights, we looked at each other. I had no wish to speak to him further, and left him. Besides, he was going away soon.

After this, everything was dull and empty again. I went out alone, aping myself and shouting: "Bricks for the palace! The calf is much stronger today!" And when this was done, I did other nothings, and when my money began to run out, I wrote to my publisher, pretending I would soon send him an unbelievably remarkable manuscript. In short, I behaved like a man in love. These were the typical symptoms.

And to take the bull by the horns: no doubt you suspect me of dwelling on the subject of Miss Torsen out of self-interest? In that case I must have concealed well in these pages that I never think of her except as an object, as a theme; turn back the pages and you will see! At my age, one does not fall in love without becoming grotesque, without making even the Pharaohs laugh.

Finis.

But there is one thing I cannot finish doing, and that is withdrawing to my room, and sitting alone with the good darkness round me. This, after all, is the last pleasure.

An interlude:

Miss Torsen and her actor are walking this way; I hear their footsteps and their voices; but since I am sitting in the dark of the evening, I cannot see them. They stop outside my open window, leaning against it, and the actor says something, asks her to do something she does not want to do, tries to draw her with him; but she resists.

Then he grows angry.

"What the devil did you send for me for?" he asks roughly.

And she begins to weep and says:

"So that's all you've come for! Oh, oh! But I'm not like that at all. Why can't you leave me alone? I'm not hurting you."

Am I one who understands women? Self-deception. Vain boasting. I made my presence known then because her weeping sounded so wretched; I moved a chair and cleared my throat.

The sound caught his attention at once, and he hushed her, trying to listen; but she said:

"No, it was nothing...."

But she knew very well this was not true; she knew what the sound was. It was not the first time Miss Torsen used this trick with me; she had often pretended that she thought I was not within hearing, and then created some such delicate situation. Each time I had promised myself not to intervene; but she had not wept before; now she wept.

Why did she use these wiles? To clear herself in my eyes—mine, the eyes of a settled man—to make me believe how good she was, how well-behaved! But, dear child, I knew that before; I could see it from your hands! You are so unnatural that in your seven and twentieth year, you walk unmarried, barren and unopen!

The pair drifted away.

And there is something else I cannot finish doing: withdrawing into solitude in the woods, alone with the good darkness round me. This is the last pleasure.

One needs solitude and darkness, not because one flees the company of others and can endure only one's own, but because of their quality of loftiness and religion. Strange how all things pass distantly, yet all is near; we sit in an omnipresence. It must be God. It must be ourselves as a part of all things.

> What would my heart, where would I stray?
> Shall I leave the forest behind me?
> It was my home but yesterday;
> now toward the city I wend my way;
> to the darkness of night I've resigned me.
> The world round me sleeps as I tarry, alone,
> soothing my ear with its quiet.
> How large and gray is the city of stone
> in which the many all hopes enthrone!
> Shall I, too, accept their fiat?
>
> Hark! Do the bells ring on the hillside?
>
> Back to the peace of the forest I turn
> in the nightly hour that's hoarest.

There's a sweet-smelling hedgerow to which I yearn;
I shall rest my head on heather and fern,
and sleep in the depths of the forest.

Hark, how the bells ring on the hillside!

Romantic? Yes. Mere sentimentality, mood, rhyme—nothing? Yes.

It is the last happiness.

XXIII

The sun has returned. Not darkly glowing and regal—more than that: imperial, because it is flaming. This you do not understand, my friend, whatever the language in which it is dished up for you. But I say there is an imperial sun in the sky.

It's a good day for going to the woods; it is sweeping time, for the woods are full of yellow things that have come suddenly into being. A short time ago they were not there, or I did not see them, or they had the earth's own complexion. There is something unborn about them, like embryos in an early stage. But if I whirl them about, they are miracles of fulfillment.

Here are fungi of every sort, mushrooms and puffballs. How close is the poisonous mushroom to the happy family of the edible mushroom, and how innocently it stands there! Yet it is deadly. What magnificent cunning! A spurious fruit, a criminal, habitual vice itself, but preening in splendor and brilliance, a very cardinal of fungi. I break off a morsel to chew; it is good and soft on the tongue, but I am a coward and spit it out again. Was it not the poisonous mushroom that drove men berserker? But in the dawn of our own day, we die of a hair in the throat.

The sun is already setting. Far up the mountainside are the cattle, but they are moving homeward now; I can hear by their bells that they are moving. Tinkling bells and deep-mouthed bells, sometimes sounding together as though there were a meaning in it, a pattern of tones, a rapture.

And rapture, too, to see all the blades of grass and the tiny flowers and plants. Beside me where I lie is a small pod plant, wonderfully meek, with tiny seeds pushing out of the pod—God bless it, it's becoming a mother! It has got caught in a dry twig and I liberate it. Life quivers within it; the sun has warmed it today and called it to its destiny. A tiny, gigantic miracle.

Now it is sunset, and the woods bend under a rustling that passes through them sweet and heavy; it is the evening.

I lie for another hour or two; the birds have long since gone to rest, and darkness falls thick and soft.... As I walk homeward, my feet feel their way and I hold my hands before me till I reach the field, where it is a little lighter. I walk on the hay that has been left outdoors; it is tough and black, and I slip on it because it is already rotting. As I approach the houses, bats fly noiselessly past me, as though on wings of foam. A slight shudder convulses me whenever they pass.

Suddenly I stop.

A man is walking here. I can see him against the wall of the new house. He has on a coat that looks like the actor's raincoat, but it is not the little comedian himself. There he goes, into the house, right into the house. It is Solem.

"Why, that's where she sleeps!" I think. "Ah, well. Alone in the building, in the south wing, Miss Torsen alone—yes, quite alone. And Solem has just gone in."

I stand there waiting to be at hand, to rush in to the rescue, for after all I am a human being, not a brute. Several minutes pass. He has not even bothered to be very quiet, for I hear him clicking the key in the lock. Surely I ought to hear a cry now? I hear nothing, nothing; a chair scraping across the floor, that is all.

"But good heavens, he may do her some harm! He may injure her; he may overpower her with rape! Ought I not to tap on the window? I—what for? But at the very first cry, I shall be on the spot, take my word for it."

Not a single cry.

The hours pass; I have settled down to wait. Of course I cannot go my way and desert a helpless woman. But the hours wear on. A very thorough business in there, nothing niggardly about this; it is almost dawn. It occurs to me that he may be killing her, perhaps has killed her already; I am alarmed and about to get up—when the key clicks in the lock again and Solem emerges. He does not run, but walks back the way he came, down to the veranda of my own house. There he hangs the actor's raincoat where it hung before, and emerges again. But this time he is naked. He has been naked under the coat all this time. Is it possible? Why not? No inhibitions, no restraint, no covering; Solem has thought it all out. Now, stark naked, he stalks to his room.

What a man!

I sit thinking and collecting myself and regaining my wits. What has happened? The south wing is still wrapped in silence, but the lady is not dead; I can see that from Solem's fearless manner as he goes to his room, lights the lamp, and goes to bed.

It relieves me to know she is alive, revives me, and makes me superlatively brave: if he has dared to kill her, I will report it at once. I shall not spare him. I shall accuse him of both her death and the lawyer's. I shall go further: I shall accuse others—the thief of last winter, the man that stole the sides of bacon from a tradesman and sold me rolls of tobacco out of his bag. No, I shall not keep silence about anything then....

XXIV

When it grew light, Solem went to the kitchen, had his breakfast, settled his business with Paul and the women, and returned to his room. He was in no hurry; though it was no longer early in the day, he took his time about tying his bundles, preparatory to leaving. Lingeringly he looked into the windows of the south wing as he passed.

Then Solem was gone.

A little later Miss Torsen came in to breakfast. She asked at once about Solem. And why might she be so interested in Solem? She had certainly stopped in her room intentionally so as to give him time to leave; if she wanted to see him she could have been here long ago.

81

But was it not safest to seem a little angry? Supposing, night owl that I was, that I had seen something!

"Where is Solem?" she asked indignantly.

"Solem has gone now," Josephine replied.

"Lucky for him!"

"Why?" asked Josephine.

"Oh, he's a dreadful creature!"

How agitated she was! But in the course of the day she calmed down. Her anger dissolved, and there was neither weeping nor a scene; only she did not walk proudly, as was her habit, but preferred to sit in silence.

That passed too; she roused herself briskly soon after Solem's departure, and in a few days she was the same as ever. She took walks, she talked and laughed with us, she made the actor swing her in the children's swing, as in the lawyer's day....

I went out one evening, for there was good weather and darkness for walking; there was neither a moon nor stars. The gentle ripple of the little Reisa river was all the sound I heard; there were God and Goethe and über allen Gipfeln ist Ruh' that night. On my return, I was in the mood to walk softly and on tiptoe, so I undressed and went to bed in the dark.

Then they came again to my window, those two lunatics, the lady and the actor. What next? But it was not he that chose this spot; of that I was sure. She chose it because she was convinced I had returned. There was something she wanted me to hear.

Why should I listen to him still pleading with her?

"I've had enough of this," he said. "I'm leaving tomorrow."

"Oh, well...." she said. "No, let's not tonight," she added suddenly; "some other time. Yes? In a few days? We'll talk about it tomorrow. Good night."

For the first time it struck me: she wants to rouse you, too, settled man though you are; she wants to make you as mad as the others! That's what she's after!

82

And now I remember, before the lawyer arrived, when there was Tradesman Batt—I remember how during his first few days here, she would give me a kind word or a look that was quite out of the picture, and as unmistakable as her pride would permit. No, she had no objections to seeing old age wriggle. And listen to this: before this she had been intent to show a well-behaved indifference to sex, but that was finished; was she not at this moment resisting only faintly, and raising definite hopes? "Not tonight, but some other time," she had said. Yes, a half-refusal, a mere postponement, that I was meant to hear. She was corrupt, but she was also cunning, with the cunning of a madman. So corrupt.

Dear child, Pharaoh laughs before his pyramids; standing before his pyramids he laughs. He would laugh at me, too.

Next day we three remaining guests were sitting in the living room. The lady and the actor read one book; I read another.

"Will you," she says to him, "do me a great favor?"

"With pleasure."

"Would you go out in the grounds where we sat yesterday and fetch my galoshes?"

So he went out to do her this great favor. He sang a well-known popular song as he crossed the yard, cheerful in his own peculiar way.

She turned to me.

"You seem silent."

"Do I?"

"Yes, you're very silent."

"Listen to this," I said, and began to read to her from the book I held in my hands. I read a longish bit.

She tried to interrupt me several times, and at length said impatiently:

"What is this you want me to listen to?"

"The Musketeers. You must admit it's entertaining."

"I've read it," she said. And then she began to clasp her hands and drag them apart again.

"Then you must hear something you haven't read before," I replied, and went across to my room to fetch a few pages I had written. They were only a few poems—nothing special, just a few small verses. Not that I am in the habit of reading such things aloud, but I seized on this for the moment because I wanted to prevent her from humbling herself, and telling me anything more.

While I was reading the poems to her, the actor returned.

"I couldn't find any galoshes there," he said.

"No?" she replied absently.

"No, I really looked everywhere, but...."

She got up and left the room.

He looked after her in some surprise, and sat still for a moment. Then it occurred to him.

"I believe her galoshes are in the passage outside her door," he said, and hurried after her.

I sat back, thinking it over. There had been a sweetness in her face as she said, "Yes, you're very silent." Had she seen through me and my pretext for reading to her? Of course she had. She was no fool. I was the fool, nobody else. I should have driven a sportsman to despair. Some practice the sport of making conquests and the sport of making love, because they find it so agreeable; I have never practiced sport of any kind. I have loved and raged and suffered and stormed according to my nature—that is all; I am an old-fashioned man. And here I sit in the shadow of evening, the shadow of the half-century. Let me have done!

The actor returned to the living room confused and dejected. She had turned him out; she had wept.

I was not surprised, for it was the mode of expression of her type.

"Have you ever heard the like of it? She told me to get out! I shall leave tomorrow."

"Have you found the galoshes?" I asked.

"Of course," he replied. "They were right in the passage. 'Here they are,' I said to her. 'Yes, yes,' she said. 'Right under your nose,' I said. 'Yes, yes, go away,' she said, and began to cry. So I went away."

"She'll get over it."

"Do you think so? Yes, I expect she will. Oh, well, it's my opinion nobody can understand women, anyhow. But they're a mighty sex, the women, a mighty sex. They certainly are."

He sat on a while, but he had no peace of mind, and soon went out again.

That evening the lady was in the dining room before us; she was there when we came in, and we all nodded slightly in greeting. To the actor she was very kind, quite making up for her petulance of the afternoon.

When he sat down he found a letter in his table napkin: a written note folded into the napkin. He was so surprised that he dropped everything he was doing to unfold and read it. With an exclamation and a smile, his blue, delighted eyes splashed over her; but she was looking down into her lap with her forehead wrinkled, so he put the note away in his vest pocket.

Then it probably dawned on him that he had betrayed her, and he tried to cover it up somehow.

"Well, here goes for food!" he said, as though he were going to require all his energy for the task of eating.

Why had she written? There was nothing to prevent her speaking to him. He had, after all, been sitting on the doorstep when she emerged from her room and passed him. Had she foreseen that the good comedian could not contain himself, but would surely let a third person into the secret?

Why probe or question further? The actor did not eat much, but he looked very happy. So the note must have said yes, must have been a promise; perhaps she would not tantalize him further.

XXV

A few days later, they were going to leave. They would travel together, and that would be the end.

I might have pitied them both, for though life is good, life is stern. One result at any rate was accomplished. She had not sent for him in vain, nor had he come in vain.

That was the end of the act. But there were more acts to come— many more.

She had lost much: having been ravished, she gave herself away; why be niggardly now? And this is the destiny of her type, that they lose increasingly much, retaining ever less; what need to hold back now? The ground has been completely shifted: from half-measures to the immolation of all virtue. The type is well-known, and can be found at resorts and boarding-houses, where it grows and flourishes.

In spite of her wasted adolescence, her examination and her "independence," she has been coming home from her office stool or her teacher's desk more or less exhausted; suddenly she finds herself in the midst of a sweet and unlimited idleness, with quantities of tinned food for her meals. The company round her is continually changing, tourists come and go, and she passes from hand to hand for walks and talks; the tone is "country informality." This is sheer loose living; this is a life stripped of all purpose. She does not even sleep enough because she hears through the thin wall every sound made by her neighbor in the next room, while arriving or departing Englishmen bang doors all night. In a short time she has become a neurotic, sated with company, surfeited with herself and the place. She is ready to go off with the next halfway respectable organ grinder that happens along. And so she pairs off with the most casual visitors, flirts with the guide, hovering about him and making bandages for his fingers, and at last throws herself into the arms of a nameless nobody who has arrived at the house today.

This is the Torsen type.

And now, at this very moment, she retires to her room to collect the fragments of herself, in preparation for her departure—at the end of the summer. It takes time; there are so many fragments, one in every corner. But perhaps it consoles her to think that she knows the genitive of mensa.

Things are not quite so bad for the actor. He has staked nothing, is committed to nothing. No part of his life is destroyed, nor anything within him. As he came, so he goes, cheerful, empty, nice. In fact he is even something more of a man because he has really made a conquest. He has no wish but to spend some pleasant hours with the Torsen type.

He strolled about the garden waiting for her to get ready. Once she was visible through the doorway, and he called to her:

"Aren't you coming soon? Don't forget we've got to cross the mountain!"

"Well, I can't go bareheaded," she replied.

He was impatient.

"No, you've got to put your hat on, and what a lot of time that takes! Ugh!"

She measured him coldly and said:

"You're very—familiar."

If he had paid her back in the same coin there would have been weeping and gnashing of teeth and cries of "Go away! Go alone!" and an hour's delay, and reconciliation and embraces. But the actor's manner changed at once, and he replied docilely, as his nature was,

"Familiar? Well—perhaps. Sorry!"

Then he strolled about the garden again, humming occasionally and swinging his stick. I took note of the oddly feminine shape of his knees, and the unusual plumpness of his thighs; there was something unnatural about this plumpness, as though it did not belong to his sex.

His shoes were down at the heel, and his collar was open. His raincoat hung regally from his shoulders and flapped in the wind, though it was not raining. He was a proud and comical sight. But why speak harsh words about a raincoat? It was not he, the owner, that had abused it, and it hung from his shoulders as innocently as a bridal veil.

Why speak harsh words about anyone? Life is good, but life is stern. Perhaps when she comes out, I think to myself, the following scene will take place: I stand here waiting only for this departure. So she gives me her hand and says good-bye.

"Why don't you say something?" she asks in order to seem bright and easy in her mind.

"Because I don't want to hurt you in the great error of your ways."

"Ha, ha, ha," she laughs, too loudly and in a forced tone; "the great error of my ways! Well, really!"

And her anger grows, while I am assured and fatherly, standing on the firm ground of conscious virtue. Yet I say an unworthy thing like this:

"Don't throw yourself away, Miss Torsen!"

She raises her head then; yes, the Torsen type would raise her head and reply, pale and offended:

"Throw myself away?—I don't understand you."

But it is possible, too, that Miss Torsen, at heart a fine, proud girl, would have a lucid moment and see things in their true light:

"Why not, why shouldn't I throw myself away? What is there to keep? I am thrown away, wasted ever since my school days, and now I am seven and twenty...."

My own thoughts run away with me as I stand there wishing I were somewhere else. Perhaps she, too, in her room wishes me far away.

"Good-bye," I say to the actor. "Will you remember me to Miss Torsen? I must go now."

"Good-bye," says he, shaking hands in some surprise. "Can't you wait a few minutes? Well, all right, I'll give her your greeting. Good-bye, good-bye."

I take a short cut to get out of the way, and as I know every nook and corner, I am soon outside the farm, and find a good shelter.

88

From here I shall see when these two leave. She has only to say good-bye now to the people of the farm.

It struck me that yesterday was the last time I spoke to her. We spoke only a few insignificant words that I have forgotten, and today I have not spoken to her....

Here they come.

Curious—they seemed somehow to have become welded together; though they walked separately up the mountain track, yet they belonged together. They did not speak; the essential things had probably already been said. Life had grown ordinary for them; it still remained to them to be of use to each other. He walked first, while she followed many paces behind; it was lonely to look at against the rugged background of the mountain. Where had her tall figure gone to? She seemed to have grown shorter because she had hitched up her skirt and was carrying her knapsack on her back. They each carried one, but he carried hers and she his, probably because, owing to the greater number of her clothes, hers was the heavier sack. Thus had they shifted their burdens; what burdens would they carry in the future? She was, after all, no longer a schoolmistress, and perhaps he was no longer with the theater or the films.

I watched those two crossing rocky, mountainous ground, bare ground, with not a tree anywhere except a few stunted junipers; far away near the ridge murmured the little Reisa. Those two had put their possessions together, were walking together; at the next halt they would be man and wife, and take only one room because it was cheaper.

Suddenly I started up and, moved by some impulse of human sympathy—nay, of duty—I wanted to run across to her, talk to her, say a word of warning: "Don't go on!" I could have done it in a few minutes—a good deed, a duty....

They disappeared behind the shoulder of the hill.

Her name was Ingeborg.

XXVI

And now I, too, must wander on again, for I am the last at the Tore Peak farm. The season is wearing on, and this morning it snowed for the first time—wet, sad snow.

It is very quiet at the farm now, and Josephine might have played the piano again and been friendly to the last guest; but now I am leaving, too. Besides, Josephine has little to play and be cheerful for; things have gone badly this year, and may grow worse as time goes on. The prospect is not a good one. "But something will turn up," says Josephine. She need not worry, for she has money in the bank, and no doubt there is a young man in the offing, on the other side of the fjeld.

Oh, yes, Josephine will always manage; she thinks of everything. The other day, for instance—when Miss Torsen and her friend left. The friend could not pay his bill, and all he said was that he had expected money, but it hadn't come, and he couldn't stay any longer because of his private affairs. That was all very well, but when would the bill be paid? Why, he would send it from the town, of course; that was where he had his money!

"But how do we know we'll get the money?—from him, anyway," said Josephine. "We've had these actor-people here before. And I didn't like the way he swanked about outside, thinking he was as good as anybody, and throwing his stick up in the air and catching it again. And then when Miss Torsen came in to say good-bye, I told her, and I wondered if she couldn't let me have the money for him. Miss Torsen was shocked, and said, 'Hasn't he paid himself?' 'No,' I said, 'he hasn't, and this year being such a bad one, we need every penny.' So then Miss Torsen said of course we should get the money; how much was it? And I told her, and she said she couldn't pay for him now, but she would see the money was sent; we could trust her for that. And I think we can, too. We'll get the money all right, if not from him. I daresay she'll send it herself...."

And Josephine went off to serve me my dinner.

Paul is on his feet now, too. Not that his step is always very steady, but at least he puts his feet to the ground. But he takes no interest in things; he does little more than feeding the horses and chopping some wood. He ought to be clearing the manure out of the summer cow houses for autumn use, but he keeps putting it off, and probably it will not be done at all. So far it hasn't mattered, but this morning's first wet snow has covered the hay outdoors and the maltreated land. And so it will remain till next spring. Poor Paul! He is an easygoing man at heart, but he pushes doggedly on against a whirlwind; sometimes he smiles to himself, knowing how useless it is to struggle—a distorted smile.

His father, the old man alone in his room, stands sometimes on his threshold, as he used to do, and reflects. He is lost in memories, for he has ninety years behind him. The many houses on the farm confuse him a little; the roofs are all too big for him, and he is afraid they might come down and carry him off. Once he asked Josephine if it was right that his hands and fingers should run away from him every day across the fields. So they put mittens on his hands, but he took to chewing them; in fact he ate everything he was given, and enjoyed a good digestion. So they must be thankful he had his health, Josephine said, and could be up and about.

I did not follow the others across the field, but returned the way I had come last spring, down toward the woods and the sea. It is fitting that I should go back, always back, never forward again.

I passed the hut where Solem and I had lived together, and then the Lapps—the two old people and Olga, this strange cross between a human being and a dwarf birch. A stove stood against the peat wall, and a paraffin lamp hung from the roof of their stone-age dwelling. Olga was kind and helpful, but she looked tiny and pathetic, like a ruffled hen; it pained me to watch her flit about the room, tiny and crooked, as she looked for a pair of reindeer cheeses for me.

Then I reached my own hut of last winter where I had passed so many lonely months. I did not enter it.

Or rather, I did enter it, for I had to spend the night there. But I shall skip this, so for the sake of brevity, I call it not entering. This morning I wrote something playful about Madame, the mouse I left here last spring; but tonight I am taking it out again because I am no longer in the mood, and because there is no point in it. Perhaps it would have amused you to read it, my friend; but there is no point in amusing you now. I must deject you now and make you listen to me; there is not much more to hear.

Am I moralizing? I am explaining. No, I am not moralizing; I am explaining. If it is moralizing to see the truth and tell it to you, then I am moralizing. Can I help that? Intuitively I see into what is distant; you do not, for this is something you cannot learn from your little schoolbooks. Do not let this rouse your hatred for me. I shall be merry again with you later, when my strings are tuned to merriment. I have no power over them. Now they are tuned to a chorale....

At dawn, in the bright moonlight, I leave the hut and push on quickly in order to reach the village as soon as possible. But I must have started too early or walked too fast, for at this rate I shall reach the village at high noon. What am I chasing after? Perhaps it is feeling the nearness of the sea that drives me forward. And as I stand on the last high ridge, with the glitter and roar of the sea far beneath, a sweetness darts through me like a greeting from another world. "Thalatta!" I cry; and I wipe my eyeglasses tremblingly. The roar from below is sleepless and fierce, a tone of jungle passion, a savage litany. I descend the ridge as though in a trance and reach the first house.

There was no one about, and a few children's faces at a window suddenly disappeared. Everything here was small and poor, though only the barn was of peat; the house was a timbered fisherman's home. As I entered the house, I saw that though it was as poor within as without, the floor was clean and covered with pine twigs. There were many children here. The mother was busy cooking something over the fire.

I was offered a chair, and sitting down, began to chat with a couple of small boys. As I was in no hurry and asked for nothing, the woman said:

"I expect you want a boat?"

"A boat?" I said in my turn, for I had not come by boat on my last visit; I had walked instead over fjelds and valleys many miles from the sea. "Yes, why not?" I said. "But where does it go?"

"I thought you wanted a boat to go to the trading center," she replied, "because that's where the steamer stops. We've rowed over lots of people this year."

Great changes here; the motor traffic in Stordalen must have completely altered all the other traffic since my last visit ten months ago.

"Where can I stop for a few days?" I asked.

"At the trading center, the other side of the islands. Or there's Eilert and Olaus; they're both on this side. You could go there; they've got big houses."

She showed me the two places on this side of the water, close to the shore, and I proceeded thither.

XXVII

A large house, with and upper story of planks built on later, displayed a new signboard on the wall: Room and Board. The barn, as usual, was a peat hut.

As I did not know which was Eilert and which Olaus, and had stopped to consider which road to take, a man came hurrying toward me. Ah, well, the world is a small place; we meet friends and acquaintances everywhere. Here am I, meeting an old acquaintance, the thief of last winter, the pork thief. What luck, what a satisfaction!

This was Eilert. He took in paying guests now.

At first he pretended not to recognize me, but he soon gave that up. Once he had done so, however, he carried the thing off in style:

"Well, well," he said, "what a nice surprise! You are most welcome under my humble roof, and such it is!"

My own response was rather less jaunty, and I stood still collecting my thoughts. When I had asked a few questions, he explained that since the motor traffic had started in Stordalen, many visitors came through this way, and sometimes they wanted to stop over at his house before being rowed across to the steamer. They always came down in the evenings, and it might be fine, or it might not, and at night the fjord was often wild. He had therefore had to arrange to house them, because after all, you can't expect people to spend the night outdoors.

"So you've turned into a hotelkeeper," I said.

"Well, you can joke about it," he returned, "but all I do is to give shelter to the people who come here. That's all the hotel there is to it. My neighbor Olaus can't do any more either, even if he builds a place that's ten times as big. Look over there—now he's building another house—a shed, I'd call it—and he's got three grown men working on it so he can get it done by next summer. But it won't be much bigger than my place at that, and anyhow, the gentry don't want to be bothered walking all that distance to his place when here's my house right at the car stop. And besides it was me that started it, and if I was Olaus I wouldn't have wanted to imitate me like a regular monkey and started keeping boarders which I didn't know the first thing about. But he can't make himself any different from what he is, so he puts up a few old bits of canvas and rugs and cardboard inside his barn and gets people to sleep there. But I'd never ask the gentry to sleep in a barn, a storehouse for fodder and hay for dumb beasts, if you'll excuse my mentioning it! But of course if you've no shame in you and don't know how to behave in company—"

"Lucky I've met you," I said. "Why, I might have gone on down the road to his place!"

We walked on together, with Eilert talking and explaining all the way, and assuring me over and over again that Olaus was a good-for-nothing for copying him as he did.

If I had known what was awaiting me, I should certainly have passed by Eilert's house. But I did not know. I was innocent, though I may not have appeared so. It cannot be helped.

"It's too bad I've got somebody in the best room," said Eilert. "They're gentlefolk from the city. They came down here through Stordalen, and they had to walk because the cars have stopped for the season. They've been in my house for quite some days, and I think they'll be staying on a while yet. I think they're out now, but of course it means I can't let you have my best room."

I looked up, and saw a face in the window. A shiver ran through me—no, of course not a shiver, far from it, but certainly this was a fresh surprise. What a coincidence! As we were about to enter the door, there was the actor, too—standing there looking at me: the actor from the Tore Peak resort. It was his knees, his coat, and his stick. So I was right—I had recognized her face at an upper window. Yes, indeed, the world is small.

The actor and I greeted each other and began to talk. How nice to see me again! And how was Paul, the good fellow—still soaking himself in liquor, he supposed? Funny effect it has sometimes; Paul seemed to think the whole inn was an aquarium and we visitors the goldfish! "Ha, ha, ha, goldfish; I wish we were, I must say!—Well, Eilert, are we getting some fresh haddock for supper? Good!— Really, we like it here very much; we've already been here several days; we want to stay and get a good rest."

As we stood there, a rather stout girl came down from the loft and addressed the actor:

"The missis wants you to come right upstairs."

"Oh? Very well, at once.... Well, see you later. You'll be stopping here, too, I expect?"

He hurried up the stairs.

Eilert and I followed to my room.

As a matter of fact, I went out again with Eilert at once. He had a great deal to tell me and explain to me, and I was not unwilling to listen to him then. Really, Eilert was not too bad, a fine fellow with four ragged, magnificent youngsters by his first wife, who had died two years before, and another child by his second wife. He must have forgotten, as he told me this, the yarn about the sick wife and the ailing children that he had spun for me last winter. The girl who had come down the stairs with the message from the "missis" was no servant, but Eilert's young wife. And she, too, was all right— strong and good, handy about the stables, and pregnant again.

It all looks good to me, Eilert: your wife and everything you tell me about your family.

No one will understand my strange contentment, then; I had been full of an obscure happiness from the moment I came to this house. Probably a mere coincidence, but that did not detract from my satisfactory state of mind; I was pleased with everything, and all things added to my cheerful frame of mind. There were some pigs by the barn, very affectionate pigs, because they were used to the children playing with them and kissing them and riding on their backs. And there was one of the goats, up on the roof of course, standing so far out along the edge that it was a wonder he didn't grow dizzy. Seagulls flew criss-cross over the fields, screaming their own language to one another, and being friends or enemies to the best of their ability. Down by the mouth of the river, just beneath the sunset, began the great road that winds up through the woods and the valley. There is something of the friendliness of a living being about such a forest road.

Eilert was going out in his boat to fish haddock, and I went with him. Actually he should have been getting some meat for us; but he had promised the gentry from the city some fish, and fish was one of the gifts of God. Besides, if he lacked meat, he could always slaughter one of the pigs.

There was a slight wind; but then we wanted some wind, Eilert said, as long as there was not too much of it.

"Not reliable tonight though," he said, looking up into the sky; "the bigger the wind, the stronger the current."

At first I was very brave, and sat on the thwart thinking of Eilert's French words: travali, prekevary, sutinary, mankémang, and many others. They've had a long way to travel, coming here by ancient routes via Bergen, and now they're common property.

And then suddenly I lost all interest in French words, and felt extremely ill. It was much too windy, and we got no haddock.

"Pity she's come up so quick," said Eilert; "let's try inshore for a while."

But we got nothing there either, and as the wind increased and the sea rose, "We'd better go home," said Eilert.

The sea had been just right before, remarkably so, but now there was entirely too much of it. Why on earth did I feel so bad? An inner exhaustion, some emotional excitement, would have explained it. But I had experienced no emotional excitement.

We rowed in the foam and feathery jets of spray. "She's rising fast!" cried Eilert, rowing with all his might.

I felt so wretched that Eilert told me to ship my oars; he would manage by himself. But for all my wretchedness, I remembered that they could see me from the shore, and I would not put down my oars. Eilert's wife might see me and laugh at me.

What a revolting business, this seasickness that forced me to put my head over the gunwale and make a pig of myself! I had a moment's relief, and then it began all over again. Charming! I felt as though I were in labor; the wrong way up, of course, through my throat, but it was a delivery nonetheless. It moved up, then stopped, came on again and stopped, came on and stopped once more. It was a lump of iron—iron, did I say? No, steel; I had never felt anything like it before; it was not something I was born with. All my internal mechanism was stopped by it. Then I took a running start far down inside me and began, strangely, to howl with all my strength; but a howl, however successful, cannot break down a lump of steel. The pains continued. My mouth filled with bile. Soon, thank heaven, my chest would burst. O—oh—oh.... Then we rowed inside the islands that served as a breakwater, and I was saved.

Quite suddenly I was well again, and began to play the clown, imitating my own behavior in order to deceive the people ashore. And I assured Eilert, too, that this was the first time I had ever been seasick, so that he should understand it was nothing to gossip about. After all, he had not heard about the great seas I had sailed without the slightest discomfort; once I had been four-and-twenty days on the ocean, with most of the passengers in bed, and even the captain sick in cascades; but not me!

"Yes, I get seasick sometimes, too," says Eilert.

That evening I sat eating alone in the dining room. Since we had not brought back any haddock, the visitors upstairs had no desire to come down. All they wanted, Eilert's wife said, was some bread and butter and milk to be sent up.

XXVIII

Next morning they had gone.

Yes, indeed, they left at four in the morning, at dawn; I heard them perfectly well, for my room was near the stairs. The knight of the plump thighs came first, clumping heavily down the stairs. She hushed him, and her voice sounded angry.

Eilert had just risen too, and they stood outside for some minutes, negotiating with him for the boat—yes, at once; they had changed their minds and wanted to leave, immediately. Then they went down to the boat, Eilert with them. I could see them through the window, chilled by the cold of early morning and short-tempered with each other. There had been a frost during the night; ice lay on the water in the buckets, and the ground was harsh to walk on. Poor things—no food, no coffee; a windy morning, with the sea still running rather high. There they go with their knapsacks on their backs; she is still wearing her red hat.

Well, it was no concern of mine, and I lay down again, intending to sleep till about noon. Nothing was any concern of mine, except myself. I could not see the boat from my bed, so I got up again—just to while the time away—to see how far they had gone. Not very far, though both men were rowing. A little later I got up and looked again—oh, yes, they were getting on. I took up my post by the window. It was really quite interesting to watch the boat getting smaller and smaller; finally I opened the window, even looked through my field-glasses. As it was not yet quite light, I could not see them very clearly, but the red hat was still discernible. Then the boat disappeared behind an island. I dressed and went down. The children were all still in bed, but the wife, Regine, was up. How calmly and naturally she took everything!

"Do you know where your husband is?" I asked her.

"Yes—funny, aren't they?" she replied. "I never saw them till after they'd left—gone down to the fjord. Where do you suppose they're going? Haddock fishing?"

"Maybe," was all I said. But I thought to myself: "They're leaving, all right. They had their knapsacks on their backs."

"Funny couple," Regine resumed. "Nothing to eat, no coffee, not a thing! And the missis not wanting anything to eat last night, neither!"

I merely shook my head and went out. Regine called to me that coffee was nearly ready, so if I'd like a cup—

Of course the only thing I could do in the face of such foolishness was to shake my head and go away. One must take the sensible view. How was it possible to understand such behavior? Nevertheless I, the undersigned, should have gone on to Olaus yesterday, instead of going fishing. That would have been still more sensible. What business had I at this house? Very likely she found it embarrassing to be called the "missis," and this was why she could neither eat last night nor stay here today. So she had beaten a retreat, with her friend and her knapsack.

Well, it was not much to go away with, but perhaps that doesn't matter. As long as one has a reason to go away.

Later in the forenoon Eilert returned home. He was alone, but he came up the path carrying one of the knapsacks—the larger one. He was in a furious temper, and kept saying they'd better not try it on him—no, they'd just better not.

Of course it was the bill again.

"She'll probably have a good deal of this sort of trouble," I thought to myself, "but no doubt she'll get used to it, and take it as nonchalantly as it should be taken. There are worse things."

But the fact remains that it was I that upset them, I that had driven them away without their clothes; perhaps they had really expected some money to be sent here—who knows?

I got hold of Eilert. How big was the bill? What, was that all? "Good heavens! Here you are, here's your money; now row across to them at once with their clothes!"

But it all proved in vain, for the strangers had gone; they had arrived just in time for the boat, and were aboard it at that very moment.

Well, there was no help for it.

"Here's their address," says Eilert. "We can send the clothes next Thursday; that's the next trip the boat goes south again."

I took down the address, but I was most ungracious to Eilert. Why couldn't he have kept the other knapsack—why this particular one?

Eilert replied that it was true the gentleman had offered him the other one, but he could see from the outside that it was not so good as this one. And I should remember that the money the missis had paid him hadn't covered more than the bill for one of them. So it was only reasonable that he should take the fullest knapsack. As a matter of fact, he had behaved very well, and that was the truth.

Because when she gave him the larger knapsack, and wrote the address, she had scolded, but he had kept quiet, and said not another word. And anyway, nobody had better try it on him—they'd better not, or he'd know the reason why!

Eilert shook a long-armed fist at the sky.

When he had eaten, drunk his coffee, and rested for a while, he was not so lively and talkative as on the previous day. He had been brooding and speculating ever since last summer, when the motor traffic started, and did I think it would be a good idea for him to hire three grown men, too, and build a much bigger house than Olaus's?

So he had caught it, too—the great, modern Norwegian disease!

The knapsack was back in her room again; yes, these were her clothes; I recognized her blouses, her skirts and her shoes. I hardly looked at them, of course; just unpacked them, folded them neatly, and put them back in the bag again; because no doubt Eilert had had them all out in a heap. This was really my only reason for unpacking them.

XXIX

Once more I was run into a party of English, the last for this year.

They arrived by steamer in the morning and stopped at the trading station for a few hours, meanwhile sending up a detachment through the valley to order a car to meet them. Stordalen, Stordalen, they said. So they had apparently not yet seen Stordalen—an omission they must repair at once.

And what a sensation they made!

They came across by rowboat from the trading station; we could hear them a long way off, an old man's voice drowning out all the others. Eilert dropped everything he had in hand, and ran down to the landing place in order to be the first on the spot. From Olaus's house, too, a man and a few half-grown boys went down, and from all the houses round swarmed curious and helpful crowds. There were so many spectators at the landing place that the old man with the loud voice drew himself up to his full height in the boat and majestically shouted his English at us, as though his language must of course be ours as well:

"Where's the car? Bring the car down!"

Olaus, who was sharp, guessed what he meant and at once sent his two boys up the valley to meet the car and hurry it on, for the Englishmen had arrived.

They disembarked, they were in a great hurry, they could not understand why the car had not come to meet them: "What was the meaning of this?" There were four of them. "Stordalen!" they said. As they came up past Eilert's house, they looked at their watches and swore because so many minutes were being wasted. Where the devil was the car? The populace followed at some distance, gazing with reverence on these dressed-up fools.

I remember a couple of them: an old man—the one with the loud voice—who wore a pleated kilt on each thigh and a jacket of green canvas with braid and buckles and straps and innumerable pockets all over it. What a man, what a power! His beard, streaming out from under his nose like the northern lights, was greenish-white, and he swore like a madman. Another of the party was tall and bent, a flagpole of sorts, astonishing, stupendous, with sloping shoulders, a tiny cap perched above extravagantly arched eyebrows; he was an upended Roman battering ram, a man on stilts. I measured him with my eyes, and still there was something left over. Yet he was bent and broken, old before his time, quite bald; but his mouth was tight as a tiger's, and he had a madness in his head that kept him on the move.

"Stordalen!" he cried.

England will soon have to open old people's homes for her sons. She desexes her people with sport and obsessive ideas: were not other countries keeping her in perpetual unrest, she would in a couple of generations be converted to pederasty....

Then the horn of the car was heard tooting in the woods, and everyone raced to meet it.

Of course Olaus's two boys had done an honest day's work in meeting the car so far up the road, and urging the driver to hurry; were they not to get any reward? True, they were allowed to sit in the back seat for their return journey and thus enjoyed the drive of a lifetime; but money! They had acquired enough brazenness in the course of the summer not to hesitate, and approached the loud-voiced old man, holding out their palms and clamoring: "Money!" But that did not suit the old man, who entered the car forthwith, urging his companions to hurry. The driver, no doubt thinking of his own tips, felt he would serve his passengers best by driving off with them at once. So off he went. A toot of the horn, and a rapid fanfare—tara-ra-boom-de-ay!

The spectators turned homeward, talking about the illustrious visitors. Foreign lands—ah, no, this country will not bear comparison with them! "Did you see how tall the younger lord was?" "And did you see the other one, the one with the skirts and the northern lights?"

But some of the homeward-turning bumpkins, such as the Olaus family, had more serious matters on their minds. Olaus for the first time understood what he had read in the paper so many times, that the Norwegian elementary school is a worthless institution because it does not teach English to the children of the lower orders. Here were his boys, losing a handsome tip merely because they could not swear back intelligibly at the gentleman with the northern lights. The boys themselves had also something to think about: "That driver, that scoundrel, that southerner! But just wait!" They had heard that bits of broken bottle were very good for tires....

I return to her knapsack and her clothes, and the reason why I do so is that Eilert is so little to be trusted. I want to count her clothes to make sure none of them disappear; it was a mistake not to have done so at once.

It may seem as though I kept returning to these clothes and thinking about them; but why should I do that? At any rate it is now evident that I was right in suspecting Eilert, for I heard him going upstairs, and when I came in, he was turning out the bag and going through the clothes.

"What are you doing?" I said.

At first he tried to brazen it out.

"Never you mind," he replied. But my knowing something about him was so much to my advantage that he soon drew in his horns. How I wronged him, he complained, and exploited him:

"You haven't bought these clothes," he said. "I could have got more for them if I'd sold them." He had been paid, but he still wanted more, like the stomach, which goes on digesting after death. That was Eilert. Yet he was not too bad; he had never been any better, and he certainly had grown no worse with his new livelihood.

May no one ever grow worse with a new livelihood!

So I moved the knapsack and the clothes into my own room in order to take better care of them. It was a slow job to tidy everything up for the second time, but it had to be done. Later that evening I would resume my journey, taking the knapsack with me. I had done with the place, and the nights were moonlit again.

Enough of these clothes!

XXX

Once again I am at an age when I walk in the moonlight. Thirty years ago I walked in the moonlight, too, walked on crackling, snowy roads, on bare, frozen ground, round unlocked barns, on the hunt for love. How well I remember it! But it is no longer the same moonlight. I could even read by it the letter she gave me. But there are no such letters any more.

Everything is changed. The tale is told, and tonight I walk abroad on an errand of the head, not of the heart: I shall go across to the trading center and dispatch a knapsack by the steamer; after that I shall wander on. And that requires nothing but a little ordinary training in walking, and the light of the moon to see by. But in those old days, those young days, we studied the almanac in the autumn to find out if there would be a moon on Twelfth Night, for we could use it then.

Everything is changed; I am changed. The tale lies within the teller.

They say that old age has other pleasures which youth has not: deeper pleasures, more lasting pleasures. That is a lie. Yes, you have read right: that is a lie. Only old age itself says this, in a self-interest that flaunts its very rags. The old man has forgotten when he stood on the summit, forgotten his own self, his own alias, red and white, blowing a golden horn. Now he stands no longer—no, he sits—it is less of a strain to sit. But now there comes to him, slow and halting, fat and stupid, the honor of old age. What can a sitting man do with honor? A man on his feet can use it; to a sitting man it is only a possession. But honor is meant to be used, not to be sat with.

Let sitting men wear warm stockings.

What a coincidence: another barn on my road, just as in the days of the golden horn! It offers me plenty of straw and shelter for the night; but where is the girl who gave me the letter? How warm her breath was, coming between lips a little parted! She will come again, of course; let us wait, we have plenty of time, another twenty years— oh, yes, she will come....

I must be on my guard against such traps. I have entered upon the honorable years; I am weak and quite capable of believing that a barn is a gift from above: thou well-deserving old man, here is a barn for thee!

No, thank you, I'm only just in my seventies.

And so in my errand of the head I pass by the barn.

Toward morning I find shelter under a projecting crag. It is fitting that I should live under crags hereafter, and I lie down in a huddle, small and invisible. Anything else you please, as long as you don't flaunt your selfishness and your rags!

I am comfortable now, lying with my head on another person's knapsack full of used clothes; I am doing this solely because it is just the right size. But sleep will not come; there are only thoughts and dreams and lines of poetry and sentimentality. The sack smells human, and I fling it away, laying my head on my arm. My arm smells of wood—not even wood.

But the slip of paper with the address—have I got the address? And I scratch a match to read it through and know it by heart tomorrow. Just a line in pencil, nothing; but perhaps there is a softness in the letters, a womanliness—I don't know.

It doesn't matter.

I manage to reach the trading center at midday, when everyone is up and about, and the post office open. They give me a large sheet of wrapping paper and string and sealing wax; I wrap the parcel and seal it and write on the outside. There!

Oh—I forgot the slip of paper with the address—to put it inside, I mean. Stupid! But otherwise I have done what I should. As I continue on my way, I feel strangely void and deserted; no doubt because the knapsack was quite heavy after all, and now I am well rid of it. "The last pleasure!" I think suddenly. And as I walk on I think irrelevantly: "The last country, the last island, the last pleasure...."

XXXI

What now?

I didn't know at first. The winter stood before me, my summer behind me—no task, no yearning, no ambition. As it made no difference where I stayed, I remembered a town I knew, and thought I might as well go there—why not? A man cannot forever sit by the sea, and it is not necessary to misunderstand him if he decides to leave it. So he leaves his solitude—others have done so before him—and a mild curiosity drives him to see the ships and the horses and the tiny frostbitten gardens of a certain town. When he arrives there, he begins to wonder in his idleness if he does not know someone in this town, in this terrifyingly large town. The moonlight is bright now, and it amuses him to give himself a certain address to visit evening after evening, and to take up his post there as though something depended on it. He is not expected anywhere else, so he has the time. Then one evening someone finds him reading under a lamppost, stops suddenly and stares, takes a few steps toward him, and bends forward searchingly.

"Isn't it—? Oh, no, excuse me, I thought—"

"Yes, it is. Good evening, Miss Torsen."

"Why, good evening. I thought it looked like you. Good evening. Yes, thank you, very well. And thanks for the knapsack; I understood all at once—I quite understand—"

"Do you live here? What a strange coincidence!"

105

"Yes, I live here; those are my windows. You wouldn't like to come up, would you? No, perhaps you wouldn't."

"But I know where there are some benches down by the shore. Unless you're cold?" I suggested.

"No, I'm not cold. Yes, thank you, I'd like to."

We went down to a bench, looking like a father and daughter out walking. There was nothing striking about us, and we sat the whole evening undisturbed. Later we sat undisturbed on other evenings all through a cold autumn month.

Then she told me first the short chapter of her journey home, some of it only hinted, suggested, and some of it in full; sometimes with her head deeply bowed, sometimes, when I asked a question, replying by a brief word or a shake of the head. I write it down from memory; it was important to her, and it became important for others as well.

Besides—in a hundred years it will all be forgotten. Why do we struggle? In a hundred years someone will read about it in memoirs and letters and think: "How she wriggled, how she fussed—dear me!" There are others about whom nothing at all will be written or read; life will close over them like a grave. Either way...

What sorrows she had—dear, dear, what sorrows! The day she had been unable to pay the bill, she thought herself the center of the universe; everybody stared at her, and she was at her wits' end. Then she heard a man's voice outside saying: "Haven't you watered Blakka yet?" That was his preoccupation. So she was not the center of the universe after all.

Then she and her companion had left the house, and set out on their tour. The center? Not at all. Day after day they walked across fields, and through valleys, had meals in houses by the way, and water from the brooks. If they met other travelers, they greeted them, or they did not greet them; no one was less a center of attention than they, and no one more. Her companion walked in vacant thoughtlessness, whistling as he went.

At one place they stopped for food.

"Will you pay for mine for the time being?" he said.

She hesitated and then said briefly that she could not pay "for the time being" all the way.

"Of course not, by no means," said he. "Just for the moment. Perhaps we can get a loan further down the valley."

"I don't borrow."

"Ingeborg!" said he, pretending playfully to whimper.

"What is it?"

"Nothing. Can't I say 'Ingeborg' to my own wife?"

"I'm not your own wife," she said, getting up.

"Pish! We were man and wife last night. It says so in the visitors' book."

She was silent at this. Yes, last night they had been man and wife; that was to save getting two rooms, and travel economically. But she had been very foolish to agree to it.

"'Miss Torsen,' then?" he whimpered.

And to put an end to the game, she paid for both of them and took her knapsack on her back.

They walked again. At the next stop she paid for them both without discussion—for the evening meal, for bed and breakfast. It grew to be a habit. They walked on once more. They reached the end of the valley by the sea, and here she revolted again.

"Go away—go on by yourself; I don't want you in my room any more!"

The old argument no longer held good. When he repeated that they saved money by it, she replied that she for her part required no more than one room, and was quite able to pay for it. He joked again, whimpered, "Ingeborg!" and left her. He was beaten, and his back was bent.

She ate alone that evening.

"Isn't your husband coming in?" asked the woman of the house.

"Perhaps he doesn't want anything," she replied.

There he stood, away by the tiny barn pretending to be interested in the roof, in the style of building, and walked round looking at it, pursing his lips and whistling. But she could see perfectly well from the window that his face was blue and dejected. When she had eaten, she walked down to the shore, calling as she passed him:

"Go in and eat!"

But he had not sunk quite so low; he would not go in to eat, and slept under no roof that night.

It ended as such things usually end: when she found him at last next morning, regretting her action and shaken by his appearance, everything slipped back again to where it had been.

They stopped at this place a few days, waiting for the mail boat, when one evening an elderly man came to the house. She knew him, and he knew them both; she was thrown into a state of the greatest excitement, made ready to leave at once, wept and beat her breast, and wanted to go home, immediately, at once. It ended as such things usually end: when she had calmed down, she went to bed for the night. She was not the center of the universe, and the old acquaintance who had happened to pass that way did not appear to be looking only at her. Nevertheless, she staged a sort of flight early next morning, in the gray dawn, before other people were up. This much she did.

Aboard the mail boat she met no more acquaintances, and had leisure to think things over calmly. She now broke with her companion in earnest. She had a minor disagreement with him again, for he had no ticket, and one word gave rise to the next. It was all very well for her, he said; she had her return ticket in her pocket. Besides, had he not got himself involved in all these trials and tribulations because of her letter last summer, and was she not ashamed of herself? He would not have moved a foot outside the town had it not been for that letter of hers. Then she gave him her purse and all her money and asked him to leave her. There was probably enough to buy him a ticket, and now she would be rid of him.

"Of course I shouldn't accept this, but there's no other way," he said, and left her.

She stood gazing across the water, and wondering what to do. She was in a bad way now, so very different from what she had once thought; what shame, what utter futility she had wandered into! She brooded till she was worn out; then she began to listen to what people about her were saying. Two men were huddled on benches trying to shelter from the wind; she heard one of them say he was a schoolmaster, and the other that he was an artisan. The schoolmaster did not remain seated long, but got up and swaggered toward her. She passed him in silence and took his place on the bench.

It was a raw autumn day, and it did her good to get out of the wind. The artisan probably thought this tall, well-dressed lady had a berth, but when she sat down, he moved over on his own bench. He was on the point of lighting his pipe, but stopped.

"Go on, don't mind me," she said.

So he lit it, but he was careful not to blow the smoke into her face.

He was only a youngster, a little over twenty, with thick reddish hair under his cap, and whitish eyebrows high up on his forehead. His chest was broad and flat, but his back was round and his hands massive. A great horse.

Then a tray was brought him, sandwiches and coffee, which he had evidently been waiting for; he paid, but went on smoking and let the food stand.

"Please eat," she said. "You don't mind my sitting here?"

"Not at all," he replied. He knocked out his pipe slowly, taking plenty of time over it; then sat still again.

"I don't really need anything to eat yet, either," he said.

"Oh—haven't you come far?"

"No, only last night. Where do you come from, lady?"

"From the town. I've been on holiday."

"That's what I thought," he said, nodding his head.

"I've been up at the Tore Peak farm," she added.

"The Tore Peak? So."

"Do you know it?"

"No, but I know some of the people there."

A pause.

"Josephine's there," he resumed.

"Yes. Do you know her?"

"Oh, no."

They talked a little more. The boat sailed on, and they sat there talking; it was all they had to do. She asked where he came from and what his trade was, and it seemed he was nothing important, only a paltry carpenter, and his mother had a small farm. Would the lady like a simple cup of coffee?

"Why, yes, thank you." Could she have a little of his, "just a little in the saucer?"

She poured some of the coffee into the saucer and asked for a bite of food as well. Never had food tasted so good, and when she had finished, she thanked him for that, too.

"Haven't you a berth?" he asked.

"Yes, but I'd rather stay here," she said. "If I go below, I'll be sick."

"That's what I thought. Well, now I wonder—"

With that he got up and walked slowly and heavily away. She watched his back disappearing down the companion to the lower deck.

She waited for him a long time, fearing that someone else might come and take his place. Coffee from the saucer, a good-sized sandwich with the carpenter: nothing wily or unnatural about that; this sheltered corner seemed to her like a tiny foothold in life.

There he was, coming back with more food and coffee, a whole tray in his big hands. He laughed good-naturedly at himself for walking so carefully.

She threw up her hands and overdid things a little:

"Great heavens! Really, you're much, much too kind!"

"Well, I thought since you were sitting here anyhow—"

They both ate; she grew warm and sleepy, and leaned back half-dozing. Every time she opened her eyes, she saw the carpenter lighting his pipe; he struck two or three matches at once, but he was in no hurry; they were always half burned before he put his pipe in his mouth and began to suck at it. The schoolmaster called something to him, drew his attention to something far inland, but the carpenter merely nodded and said nothing.

"I wonder if he's afraid he'll wake me," she thought.

At one stop, her former traveling companion turned up again; he had been below in the cabin.

"Aren't you coming down, Ingeborg?" he asked.

She did not reply.

The carpenter looked from one to the other.

"Miss Torsen, then!" whimpered the traveling companion playfully. He stood waiting a moment, and finally went away.

"Ingeborg," the carpenter was probably thinking. "Miss Torsen," he was thinking.

"How long will you be in the town?" she asked, getting up.

"Oh, I'll be there some time."

"What are you doing there?"

He was a little embarrassed, and since his skin was so fair, she could see at once that he reddened. He bent forward, planting his elbows on his knees before he replied.

"I want to learn a little more in my trade, be an apprentice, maybe. It all depends."

"Oh, I see."

"What do you think of it?" he asked.

"I think it's a good idea."

"Do you?"

They were on deck nearly the whole of the day, but toward evening it turned bitter cold and windy. When she had grown stiff with sitting, she got up and stamped her feet, and when she had stamped till she was tired, she sat down again. Once when she was standing a little distance away, she saw the carpenter place a parcel on the bench as though to keep her seat for her.

Her quondam traveling companion stuck his head out of a doorway, the wind blowing his hair forward over his forehead, and cried:

"Ingeborg, go below, will you!"

"Oh," she groaned. Suddenly she was seized with fury. The ship heeled over on its side as she walked toward him, and she had to take a few skips to keep her balance.

"I don't want you to talk to me again," she hissed at him. "Do you hear? I mean it, by all that's holy!"

"Good gracious!" he exclaimed and disappeared.

At about three o'clock, the carpenter turned up with coffee and sandwiches again.

"Really you mustn't be doing this all the time," she said.

He merely laughed good-naturedly again, and told her to eat if she thought it was good enough.

"We'll soon be there now," she said as she ate. "Have you someone to go to?"

"Oh, yes, I have a sister."

Slowly and thoughtfully he took another sandwich and turned it over, looking at it absently before he took a bite out of it. When he had finished one mouthful, he took another. And when he had finished that one, too, he said:

"I thought that as I'm going to stay in town over the winter, I'd better learn something. And what with the farm as well—"

"Yes, indeed."

"You think so too?"

"Oh, yes. I think so."

Why did he tell her about his private affairs? She had private affairs of her own. She thanked him for the sandwiches and got up.

As the boat drew alongside the pier, he offered her his hand and said:

"My name is Nikolai."

"Oh, yes?"

"I thought in case we meet again—Nikolai Palm—but I expect the town's too big—"

"Yes, I expect it is. Well, thanks ever so much for all your kindness. Good-bye."

XXXII

I ask Miss Torsen:

"Have you met the carpenter since?"

"What carpenter? Oh—no, I haven't. I only told you about him because he's a sort of mutual acquaintance."

"Acquaintance?"

"Yes, of yours and mine. Only indirectly, of course. He happens to be the brother of that schoolmistress Miss Palm that was at the Tore Peak farm last summer."

"Well, the world's a small place. We all belong to the same family."

"And that's why I've told you all this about him."

"But you didn't find out about this relationship on the boat, did you? So you must have met him since."

"Yes,—well, no, that is to say I've seen him a few times, but not to speak to. We just said good morning and how are you and so on. Then he said he was her brother."

"Ha, ha, ha!"

"It was just in passing, quite by accident."

This gave me a good opportunity for saying: "What a lot of things are accidental! It was an accident that I should have stopped under a particular lamppost to look up something, to read a few lines. And then you happened to live there."

"That's right."

"I expect you and the carpenter will be getting married," I said.

"Ha, ha! No, indeed, I shan't marry anyone."

"No?"

"You have to be pretty naïve to marry."

"Well, I don't know that being naïve does any harm—being not quite so clever. Where does your cleverness lead you? Only to being cheated. Because there isn't anybody who's quite clever enough."

"I should have thought being clever is just the thing to protect you against being cheated. What else would it do?"

"Exactly. What else? But the trouble is we trust our cleverness so much that we get cheated that way. Or else we let things go from bad to worse, because why should we worry? After all we've got our cleverness to help get us out of the mess!"

"Well, in that case it's pretty hopeless!"

"Relying on your cleverness—yes. That was your own opinion last summer, you know."

"Yes, I remember that. I thought—oh, I don't know. But when I came back to town again it was as though—"

A pause.

"I don't know what to think," she said.

114

"And I do because I'm old and wise. You see, Miss Torsen, in the old days people didn't think so much about cleverness and secondary schools and the right to vote; they lived their lives on a different plane, they were naïve. I wonder if that wasn't a pretty good way to live. Of course people were cheated in those days, too, but they didn't smart under it so; they bore it with greater natural strength. We have lost our healthy powers of endurance."

"It's getting cold," she said. "Shall we go home?—Yes, of course that's all quite true, but we're living in modern times. We can't change the times; I can't, at any rate; I've got to keep up with the times."

"Yes, that's what it says in the Oslo morning paper. Because it used to say so in the Neue Freie Presse. But a person with character goes his own way up to a point, even if the majority go a different way."

"Yes—well, I'm really going to tell you something now," she said, stopping. "I go to a really sensible school during the day."

"Do you?" I said.

"Only this time I'm learning housekeeping; isn't that a good thing?"

"You mean you're learning to cut sandwiches for yourself?"

"Ha, ha!"

"Well, you said you weren't going to marry!"

"Oh, I don't know."

"Very well. You marry; you settle down in his valley. But first you have to learn housekeeping so that you can make an omelette or possibly a pudding for tourists or Englishmen that pass through."

"His valley? Whose valley?"

"You'd much better go to his mother's and learn all the housekeeping you're going to need from her."

"Really, really," she said smiling as she walked on again, "you're quite on the wrong track. It isn't he—it isn't anybody."

"So much the worse for you. There ought to be somebody."

"Yes, but suppose it's not the one I want."

"Oh, yes, it will be the one you want. You're big enough and handsome enough and capable enough."

"Thank you very much, but—well. Thanks so much. Good night."

Why did she break off so suddenly and leave me so hurriedly, almost at a run? Was she crying? I should have liked to have said more, to have been wise and circumstantial and made useful suggestions, but I was left standing in a kind of stupid surprise.

Then something happened.

"We haven't seen each other for such a long time," she said, the next time we met. "I'm so glad to see you again. Shall we take a short walk? I was just—"

"Going to post a letter, I see."

"Yes, I was going to post a letter. It's only—it's not—"

We went to a newspaper office with the letter. It was evidently an advertisement; perhaps she was trying to find a situation.

As she came out of the office a gentleman greeted her. She turned a deep red, and stopped for a moment at the top of the two stone steps leading from the entrance. Her head was bent almost to her chest, as though she were looking very carefully at the steps before venturing to come down them. They greeted each other again; the stranger shook her hand, and they began to talk.

He was a man of her own age, good-looking, with a soft, fair beard, and dark eyebrows that looked as though he had blacked them. He wore a top hat, and his overcoat, which was open, was lined with silk.

I heard them mention an evening of the previous week on which they had enjoyed themselves; it had been a relaxation. There had been quite a party, first out driving, then at supper together. It was a memory they had in common. Miss Torsen didn't say much. She seemed a little embarrassed, but smiling and beautiful. I began to look at the illustrated papers displayed in the window, when suddenly the thought struck me: "Good God, she's in love!"

116

"Look, I have a suggestion," he said. Then they discussed something, agreed about something, and she nodded. After that he left her.

She came toward me slowly and in silence. I spoke to her about some of the pictures in the window. "Yes," she said, "just think!" But she gazed at them without seeing anything. Silently we walked on, and for several minutes, at least, she said nothing.

"Hans Flaten never changes," she said finally.

"Is that who it was?" I asked.

"His name's Flaten."

"Yes, I remember you mentioned the name last summer. Who is he?"

"His father's a merchant."

"But he himself?"

"His father owns the big shop in Almes Street, you know."

"Yes, but what about him; what does he do?"

"I don't know if he does anything special; he just studies. His father's so rich, you know."

I recalled old Flaten's shop in Almes Street, a good, solid countryman's shop; in the mornings the yard was always full of horses, while the owners were busy making purchases in the shop.

"He's such a man of the world," she went on. "He simply throws money about—banknotes. When he goes anywhere, the people all whisper, 'That's Flaten!'"

"He dresses as though he were a baron," I said.

"Yes," she replied, rather offended. "Yes, he dresses well—always has."

"Is that the man you want?" I asked lightly.

She was silent a moment, and then said with a resolute nod:

117

"Yes."

"What—that dandy?"

"Why not? We're old friends, we've gone to school together, spent a lot of time together. It's really based on a firm foundation. He's the only man I've ever been in love with in all my life, and it's lasted many years. Sometimes, I'll admit, I forget him, but the moment I see him again, I'm as much in love as ever. I've told him so, and we both laugh about it, but that doesn't change it. It's queer."

"Then I suppose he's too rich to marry her," I thought, and asked nothing more.

When we parted, I said:

"Where does Carpenter Nikolai work?"

"I don't know," she replied. "Oh, yes, I do know. We're near there, and I can show you if you like. What do you want to see him for?"

"Nothing. I just wondered if he's at a good place, with a competent master."

Why did I, indeed, want to see Carpenter Nikolai, the artisan? Yet I have visited him and made his acquaintance. He is a bull in stature, strong and plain-featured, a man of few words. Last Saturday we saw the town together; why, I don't know, but I suggested it myself.

I made friends with the carpenter for my own sake, because of my loneliness. I no longer went to the benches by the shore, as the weather was a little too cold, and Miss Torsen interested me very little now; she had changed so much since returning to the town. She had become more the ordinary type of girl, not in any one thing, but in general. She thought of nothing but vanities and nonsense, and seemed quite to have forgotten her last summer's wholesome, bitter view of life. Now she was back at school again, in her leisure hours meeting the gentleman named Flaten, and this occupied all of her time. Either she had no depths, or she had been vitiated in the vital years of adolescence.

"What do you expect me to do?" she asked. "Of course I'm going to school again; I've been going to school ever since I was a child. I'm no good at anything else. I can only learn—that's what I'm used to.

There isn't much I can think or do on my own, and I don't enjoy it either. So what do you expect?"

No, what could I expect?

Carpenter Nikolai went to the circus. He was not much surprised at anything he saw there, or he pretended not to be. The acrobatics on horseback—"Well, not bad, but after all—!" The tiger—"I thought tigers were much bigger!" Besides, his big, heavy head seemed preoccupied with other thoughts, and he paid little attention to the women riders who were doing their tricks.

On the way home he said:

"I ought not to ask you, I expect, but would you go to the Krone with me tomorrow evening?"

"The Krone—what's that?"

"It's a place where they dance."

"A dance hall, in other words. Where is it? Do you feel so much like dancing?"

"No, not much."

"You want to see what goes on there?"

"Yes."

"All right, I'll go."

It was on a Sunday evening, the girls' and boys' own evening, that the carpenter and I went to the dance.

He had decked himself out in a starched collar and a heavy watch chain. But he was very young, and when you are young, you look well in anything. He had such remarkable strength that it was never necessary for him to give way; this had lent him assurance and authority. If you spoke to him, he was slow to reply, and if you slapped him on the shoulder, he was slow in turning round to see who had greeted him. He was a pleasant, good-humored companion.

We went to the booking office; there was no one there, and the window was closed. Moreover a notice on the wall announced that the hall was let to a private club for the first two hours of the evening.

A few young people came along as we were standing there, read the notice, and went away again. The carpenter was unwilling to go, looked round, and went in through the gate as though looking for someone.

"We can't do anything about it," I called after him.

"No," he said. "But I wonder—?"

He crossed the yard and began to look up at all the windows.

A man came down the stairs.

"What is it?" he asked.

"My friend wanted to buy a ticket," I replied. The carpenter still showed no inclination to return from the yard.

The man approached me, and proved to be the landlord. He explained, like the notice, that a club had rented the hall for the first two hours.

"Come along, we can't get in!" I called to my companion.

But he was in no hurry, so I chatted with the landlord while waiting for him.

"Yes, it's rather an exclusive club. Only eight couples, but just the same they've hired a full orchestra—rich people, you see."

They had refreshments and plenty of champagne, and then they danced as though their lives depended on it. Why they did it? Oh, well, young people, rich and fashionable, bored by Sunday evening at home; they wanted to work off the week's idleness in two hours, so they danced. Not unusual, really.

"And of course," said the landlord, "I earn more in those two hours than in the whole of the evening otherwise. Liberal people—they don't count the pennies. And yet there's no wear and tear, because of course people like that don't dance on their heels."

The carpenter, who had come halfway back, stood listening to us.

"What sort of people are they, generally speaking?" I inquired. "Businessmen, officers, or what?"

"Excuse me, but I can't tell you that," replied the landlord. "It's a private party; that's all I can say. To-night, for instance, I don't even know who they are. The money just came by special messenger."

"It's Flaten," said the carpenter.

"Flaten—is it?" said the landlord, as though he did not know it. "Mr. Flaten has been here before; he's a fine gentleman, always in fashionable company. So it's Mr. Flaten, is it? Well, excuse me, I must have another look round the hall—"

The landlord left us.

But the carpenter followed him.

"Couldn't we look on?" he asked.

"What, at the dancing? Oh, no."

"In a corner somewhere?"

"No, I couldn't allow that. I don't even let my own wife and daughter in—nobody, not a soul. They wouldn't like it."

"Are you coming or—?" I called, as though for the last time.

"Yes, I'm coming," said the carpenter, turning back.

"So you knew about this party?" I said.

"Yes," he replied. "She talked about it last Friday."

"Who talked about it? Miss Torsen?"

"Yes. She said I might sit in the gallery."

We walked on down the street, each busy with his own thoughts—or perhaps with the same thought. I, at least, was furious.

"Really, my good Nikolai, I have no desire to buy

tickets in order to look at Mr. Flaten and his ladies!"

"No."

121

Curious idea of hers, inviting this man to watch her dance. It was preposterous, but like her. Last summer, too—did she not like a third party within hearing whenever she sailed close to the wind? A thought struck me, and I asked the carpenter as calmly as I could:

"Did Miss Torsen want me to sit in the gallery, too—did she say anything about that?"

"No," he replied.

"Didn't she say anything about me?"

"No."

"You're lying," I thought, "and I daresay she's told you to lie!" I was highly incensed, but I could not squeeze the truth out of the carpenter.

Cars rolled up behind us and stopped at the Krone. Nikolai turned and wanted to go back, but when he saw that I kept straight on, he hesitated a moment and then followed me. I heard him once sighing heavily.

We strolled the streets for an hour, while I cooled off and made myself agreeable to my companion again. We had a glass of beer together, then went to a cinema, and afterward to a shooting gallery. Finally we went to a skittle ground, where we stayed for some time. Nikolai was the first to want to leave; he looked at his watch, and was suddenly in a tearing hurry. He was hardly even willing to finish the game.

We had to pass the Krone again. The cars had gone.

"Just as I thought," said the carpenter, looking very disappointed. I believe he would have liked to be present when the party came out to enter their cars. He looked up and down the empty street and repeated, "Just as I thought!" He was suddenly anxious to go home.

"No, let's go inside," I said.

It was a big, handsome hall with a platform for the orchestra, and a throng of people on the great floor. We sat in the gallery looking on.

There was a very mixed crowd: seamen, artisans, hotel staff, shop assistants, casual workers; the ladies were apparently seamstresses, servant girls, and shopgirls, with a sprinkling of light-footed damsels who had no daytime occupation. The floor was crowded with dancers. In addition to a constable whose duty it was to intervene if necessity arose, the establishment had its own commissionaire, who walked about the hall with a stick, keeping an eye on the assembled company. As soon as a dance was finished, the gentlemen all crowded to the platform and paid ten öre. If anyone seemed to be trying to cheat, the commissionaire would tap him politely on the arm with his stick. Gentlemen who had to be tapped many times were regarded as suspicious characters, and might, as a last resource, even be expelled. Order was admirably maintained.

Waltz, mazurka, schottische, square dance, waltz. I soon noticed a man who was dancing with great assiduity, never stopping once— tall, swarthy, lively—a heartbreaker. The ladies clustered round him.

"Can that be Solem down there dominating the crowd?" I thought.

"Wouldn't you like to dance?" I asked Carpenter Nikolai.

"Oh, no," he replied with a smile.

"Then we can leave any time you like."

"All right," he said and remained seated.

"Your thoughts seem to be far away."

A long pause.

"I was thinking that I haven't a horse on my farm. I have to carry all the manure and the wood myself."

"So that's why you're so strong."

"I'll have to go home in a few days and chop wood for the winter."

"Yes, of course you will."

"I was going to say—," he persisted, and then fell silent.

"Yes?"

"No, it's no use suggesting it. I'd have liked you to come with me this winter, though—I've got a small spare room."

"Why should I go there?" Still—it wasn't a bad idea.

"It would be nice if you could," said the carpenter.

Just then I heard the name of Solem mentioned in the hall. Yes, there he was, swaggering as usual, the self-same Solem from Tore Peak. He was standing alone, in high spirits, announcing that he was Solem—"Solem, my lad." He appeared not to be in the company of any one lady, for I saw him choosing partners indiscriminately. Then he chose the wrong lady, and her partner shook his head and said no. Solem remembered that. He allowed the couple to dance the next dance, and when it was finished, approached again and bowed to the lady. Once more he was refused.

The lady's appearance was striking—sophisticated or innocent, who could tell? Ash-blonde, tall, Grecian, in a black frock without trimming. How quiet and retiring she was! Of course she was a tart, but what a gentle one—a nun of vice, with a face as pure as that of a repentant sinner. Peerless!

This was a woman for Solem.

It was after he had received his second "No" from the gentleman that he began to talk, to tell everyone that he was "Solem, my lad." But his boasts were dull: Something was going to happen; he would show them an image of sin! There was no sting in it; just old, familiar rubbish these people had heard before. The commissionaire crossed over to him and asked him to be quiet, pointing at the same time to the constable by the door. This pouring of oil on the waters was successful, for Solem himself said: "Hush, we mustn't make trouble." But he did not lose sight of the Grecian and her partner.

He allowed a few dances to pass again, himself engaging other partners to dance with. There was now a huge crowd, all the late-comers having by this time arrived. Many were crowded off the floor and had to wait, rushing to get first place in the next dance instead.

Then something happened.

A couple slipped and fell. It was Solem and his partner. As he was getting up again, he tripped up another couple—the Grecian and her partner, both of whom fell down. And Solem was so strangely clumsy as he rose that his long arms and legs brought down a third couple. In a few minutes there was a squirming heap on the floor; screams and oaths were heard, people grew angry and kicked one another, while Solem skillfully directed the disaster with sincere and wholehearted malevolence. Couple after couple met their Waterloo over those already fallen. The commissionaire poked them with his stick, exhorting them to get up; the constable himself assisted him, and the music stopped. In the meantime, Solem, acting with the better part of valor, slipped out of the room and did not return.

Gradually the fallen couples got to their feet again, rubbing their shins, dusting off their clothes, some laughing, others swearing. The Grecian lady's partner had a bleeding wound on his temple, and put his hands to his head in a daze. Questions were being asked about that—what was his name?—that tall fellow who had started all the trouble. "Solem," said some of the ladies. Threats were uttered against Solem: he was the one. "Go and find him, somebody—we'll show him!"—"Why, he couldn't help it," said the ladies.

Ah, Solem, Solem—how the ladies loved him!

But the Grecian rose from the dust as from a bath. The sand from the floor clung to her black dress, making it look as though spangled with stardust. Submissively she accepted the lot of lying under all the others, entwined in their legs, and smiled when someone pointed out to her that the comb in her Grecian knot was crushed.

XXXIII

Today, the first of October forty years ago, we drove the snowplow at home. Yes, I regret to say that I remember forty years ago.

Nothing escapes my attention yet, but everything moves past me. I sit in the gallery looking on. If Nikolai the carpenter had been observant, he would have seen my fingers closing and opening again, my absurdity augmented by affectation and grimacing. Fortunately he was a child. In the end I left it all behind me, and took my proper seat. My address is the chimney corner.

Now it is winter again, with snow over the north, and Anglo-Saxon claptrap in the town. This is my desolate period; my wheels stop, my hair stops growing, my nails stop growing, everything stops growing but the days of my life. And it is well that my days increase—from now on it is well.

Not much happens during the winter. Well, of course, Nikolai has got an overcoat for the first time in his life. He didn't really need it, he says, but he bought it because of the advertisement; and it was dear, twenty kroner, but he got it for eighteen! I am sure Nikolai is much happier about his overcoat than Flaten is about his.

But let me not forget Flaten, for something has happened to him. His friends have given him a farewell party and drunk him out of bachelordom, for he is going to marry. It is Miss Torsen who told me this; I met her by accident again under her own lamppost, and she told me then.

"And you're not wearing mourning?" I said.

"Oh, no," she said, smiling. "No, it's something I've known a long time. Besides, perhaps I'm not very faithful; I don't know."

"I think you've hit the truth there."

She looked startled.

"What do you mean?"

"I think you've changed very much since last summer. You were straight and competent then, you saw clearly, you knew what you wanted. What's happened to your tinge of bitterness? Or have you no longer reason to be bitter?"

This was all too gravely spoken, but I was like a father and meant well.

She began to walk on, her head bent in thought. Then she said something very sensible:

"Last summer I had just lost my livelihood. I'm telling you things exactly as they were. I lost my post, which was a very serious matter. This made me reflect for a time; that's true. But then—I don't know—I'm quite adult, but not adult enough. I have two sisters who are really steady; they're married and quite settled, though they're younger than I. I don't know what's wrong with me."

"Would you like to go to a concert with me?" I asked.

"Now? No, thank you, I'm not dressed for it."

A pause.

126

"But it's kind of you to ask me!" she said with sudden pleasure. "It might have been very nice, but—well, you must let me tell you about the dinner party, the banquet; what a lot of pranks they thought of!"

She was right about that; these jolly young people had played a great many pranks, some of them childish and stupid, others not too bad. First they had drunk wine of the vintage of 1812. No, first of all, Flaten was sent an invitation, of course, and it consisted of a painting, a very emancipated painting in a frame, the only written words being the date and the place, and the legend: Ballads, Bachiads, Offenbachiads, Bacchanales. Then there were speeches for him who was about to leave them, and generally speaking a most deafening shouting over the wineglasses. And there was music, with someone of the company playing all the time.

But as the evening wore on, this sort of thing was not enough, and girls with their faces masked were brought in to dance. As there had been a great deal of champagne, however, this part of the program tended to deteriorate into something different, and the girls had to be sent away. Then the gentlemen went down to the hotel lobby and stood at the door watching for "opportunities."

There—a young woman approached carrying a baby and a bundle of clothes. Great, wet flakes of snow were drifting down, and she bent forward over the child to shelter it as she walked.

"Whoa!" said the gentleman and caught hold of her. "Is that your child!"

"Yes, he's mine."

"What, a boy?"

"Yes."

They talked more with her; she was thin and young, evidently a servant girl. They also looked at the child, and Helgesen and Lind, who were both short-sighted, polished their glasses and inspected it carefully.

"Are you going off to drown the child?" somebody says.

"No," says the girl in confusion.

That was a nasty question, all the others agreed, and the first one admitted it. He went off to fetch his raincoat, and hung it over the girl's shoulders. Then he tickled the child under the chin and made it smile—a marvel of a child, human bones and rags and dirt all in one little bundle.

"Poor bastard," he said. "Born of a maiden!"

"That's better!" the others remarked. "Now let's do something," they said. "Where do you live?" to the girl.

"I've lived at such and such places," she replied. "Have lived; very well, this is what we'll do," one of them said, taking out his pocketbook. The others followed suit, and a great deal of money was pushed into the girl's hand.

"Wait a minute—wait—I haven't given her enough; I asked her such a nasty question," said the first of them.

"Neither have I," said another, "because we all thought the same thing, but now we're going to settle some money on this son of a maiden!"

A collection was taken up, with Helgesen as the cashier. Then Bengt hailed a cab, invited the girl to enter, and got in after her.

"Go ahead—I want to go to Langes Street!" he called to the driver.

Bengt was taking the child home to his mother, the others said. The group were rather silent after this.

"Your eyes are so ridiculously wet, Bolt; are you crying about the money?"

"What about you?" Bolt replied. "You're as sentimental as an old woman!"

They grew cheerful again, and there were further "opportunities." A peasant came down the street with a cow he was taking to the butcher's.

"What will you charge for letting our guest of honor ride your cow?" young Rolandsen asked him. The peasant smiled and shook his head. So they bought the cow from him, paying cash for it. "Wait a minute," they said to the peasant. Then they put a label on the cow, addressed to a lady they knew.

128

"Take it to this address," they said to the peasant.

By the time they had finished with this, Bengt had returned.

"Where have you been?" they asked in surprise.

"The old lady said yes," was all he replied.

"Hurrah!" they all shouted. "Let's drink to the baby! Here, let's go to the bar. Did she really say yes? Hurrah for the old lady, too! What are we standing here for? Let's walk into the bar!"

"Walk!" someone mocks. "No, indeed, we'll drive-waiter, cars!"

The waiter rushed inside to telephone. It took some time, as it was getting late, but the gentlemen waited. It was already closing time and people were streaming out of the bar. At length the cars arrived, ten of them, one for each man. The gentlemen entered them.

"Where to?" asked the drivers.

"Next door," they said.

So the cars drove up to the next door of the same house, that being the bar, and there the gentlemen gravely got out and paid the drivers.

The bar was closed.

"Shall we break in?" they said.

"Of course," they said.

So they all ran against the door together, till it said ump! and flew open. The night watchman rushed at them, shouting, and they caught hold of him, slapped him on the back, and embraced him. Then they went behind the counter and got out bottles for him and for themselves, drinking and shouting hurrah for the baby, for Bengt's mother, for the baby's mother, for the night watchman, for love and for life. When they had done, they put some banknotes over the night watchman's mouth and tied a handkerchief over them. Then they went back to the dining room.

The supper was served. Flaten's plate was a red silk bedroom slipper lined with glass. They ate and drank and rollicked as long as they had the strength; the hours passed, and dawn approached. Then

129

Flaten began to distribute souvenirs among them. One got his watch, another his pocketbook (which was empty), a third his tie pin. After this he went on to his shoes, giving one to each of two friends, his trousers to another, and his shirt to still another, till at length he sat there in the nude. Next they collected quilts from the hotel bedrooms to wrap him up in—red silk eiderdown quilts. Flaten fell asleep and the other nine watched over him. He slept for an hour; it was morning then, and they woke him up. He started up from the quilts, found he was naked, and sent home for some more clothes. And then the party began all over again....

Later we were discussing Miss Torsen's story; she had forgotten one or two details which she filled in afterwards.

"Anyhow, it was lucky for the girl with the baby," she said.

"And for the baby itself," I said.

"Yes. But what an idea! Poor old lady, to be told such a tale!"

"Some day perhaps you'll change your mind about that."

"You think so? But it would have been nicer still if I'd got the money they settled on the child."

"You'll change your mind about that, too."

"Shall I? Why? When?"

"When you yourself have a baby that smiles at you."

"Ugh, how can you say such things!"

She must have misunderstood my meaning, for she was childishly offended. To restore her to good humor I asked at random:

"What sort of food did you get at the party?"

"Don't know," she replied.

"Don't you know?"

"Good lord, no—I wasn't there," she returned in the greatest amazement.

"Well, no, of course not, I only thought—"

"Oh, so that's it. That's what you thought!" she said, still more offended. And she clasped her hands as she had done in the summer, and tore them apart again.

"Really and truly, I do assure you—look here, honestly—I only thought you were taking a culinary interest. After all, you do learn cooking and such in the daytime."

"Oh, so you just make conversation with me; you adapt your speech to suit my narrow outlook!"

A pause.

"Anyhow, perhaps you're right up to a point; I might have asked about the food, only I forgot."

She seemed very irritable that evening. Would it interest her to talk about Flaten? A little apprehensively, I ventured:

"But you haven't told me whom Flaten is going to marry."

"She's not pretty at all," she replied suddenly. "What do you want to know for? You don't know her."

"I suppose Flaten will be entering his father's firm now?" I persisted.

"Oh, damn Flaten! You seem to care about him a lot more than I do! Flaten, Flaten, Flaten—how should I know if he's going to enter his father's firm!"

"I only thought once he's married—"

"But she's got money, too. No, I don't think he's going into his father's firm. He said once he wanted to edit a paper. Well, what's so funny about that?"

"I'm not laughing."

"Yes, you were. Anyhow, Flaten wants to edit a paper. And since Lind publishes a kennel journal, Flaten wants to publish a human journal, he says."

"A human journal?"

"Yes. And you ought to subscribe to it," she added suddenly, almost throwing the words into my face.

She was now in a state of excitement the cause of which I did not understand, so I remained silent, merely replying, "Ought I? Yes, perhaps I ought." Then she began to cry.

"Dear child, don't cry. I shan't torment you any more."

"You're not tormenting me."

"Yes, by talking nonsense; I don't seem to strike the right note."

"Yes, go on talking—that isn't it—I don't know—"

What could I say to her? But since there is, after all, nothing so interesting as a question about oneself, I said:

"You're nervous about something, but it will pass. Perhaps—well, not at once, of course—but perhaps it has hurt you that—well, that he's going his own way now. But remember—"

"You're wrong," she said, shaking her head. "That doesn't really mean anything to me; I was just slightly attracted to him."

"But you said he was the only one!"

"Oh—you know, you think that sort of thing sometimes. Of course I've been in love with other people, too; I can't deny that. Flaten was very nice, and took me out driving sometimes, or to a dance or something like that. And of course I was proud of his paying attention to me in spite of my having lost my post. I think I could have got a job in his father's shop but—anyhow, I'm looking for a job now."

"Are you? I hope you'll find a good one."

"That's just the point. But I'm not getting any job at all. That is, I shall in the end, of course, but—well, for instance, in old Flaten's shop—I shouldn't fit in there."

"Not very good pay either, I expect?"

"I'm sure it's not. And then—I don't know; I feel I know too much for it. That wretched academic training of mine does nothing but harm. Oh, well, let's not talk any more about me. It must be late; I'd better go."

I saw her to her door, said good night, and went home. I thought about her ceaselessly. It was wintry weather, with raw streets and an invisible sky. No, really, she's not suited for marriage. No man is served with a wife who is nothing but a student. Why has no one in the country noticed what the young women are coming to! Miss Torsen's tale of the wild party proved how accustomed she was to sitting and listening, and then herself disgorging endless tales. She had done it very well and not omitted much, but she paid attention only to the fun. A grown-up, eternal schoolgirl, one who had studied her life away.

When I reached my own door, Miss Torsen arrived there at the same time; she had been close at my heels all the way. I guessed this from the fact that she was not in the least breathless as she spoke.

"I forgot to ask you to forgive me," she said.

"My dear girl—?"

"Oh, for saying what I did. You mustn't subscribe. I'm so sorry about that. Please be kind and forgive me."

She took my hand and shook it.

In my amazement I stammered:

"It was really a very witty remark: a human journal—ha, ha! Now don't stand there and get cold; put your gloves on again. Are you walking back?"

"Yes. Good night. Forgive me for the whole evening."

"Let me take you home; why not stay a few minutes—"

"No, thank you."

She pressed my hand firmly and left me.

I suppose she wanted to spare my aging legs, damn them! Nevertheless I stole after her to see that she got home safely.

It happened that Josephine came to the town—Josephine, that spirit of labor from the Tore Peak farm. I saw her, too, for she came to pay me a visit. She had looked up my address, and I joked with her again and called her Joséfriendly.

How was everybody at Tore Peak? Josephine had good news about all of them, but she shook her head over Paul. Not that he drank much now; but he did little of anything else either, and had definitely lost interest in his work. He wanted to sell the farm. He wanted to try carting and delivery by horse cart in Stordalen. I asked if he had any prospective purchaser. Yes; Einar, one of the cotters, had had rather an eye on the farm. It all depended on Manufacturer Brede, who had put so much money into it.

I remembered her father, the old man from another world, the man with mittens, who had to be spoon-fed on porridge because he was ninety, who smelled like an unburied corpse. I remembered him and asked Josephine:

"Well, I expect your old father is dead by now?"

"No, praise be," she replied. "Father is better than we dared hope. We must be thankful he's still on his feet."

I took Josephine to the cinema and the circus, and she thought it all quite delightful. But she was shocked at the behavior of the ladies who rode with so little clothing on. She wanted to go to one of the great churches, too, and found her way there alone. For several days she was in the town and did a good deal of shopping. I never once saw her dejected or brooding about anything, and at length she said good-bye, because she was going back next day.

Oh, so she was going home?

Yes, she had done what she had come to do. She had also been to see Miss Torsen and got the money for the actor, because of course he had never sent it.

"Poor Miss Torsen! She was furious with him for not sending it, and turned quite red and ashamed, too. She didn't seem to find it very easy either, because she asked me to wait till next day, but she gave it to me then."

So Josephine had nothing more to do in the town. She had just visited Miss Palm, but she had not, on this occasion, met Miss Palm's brother, Nikolai, who was apprenticed to a master carpenter. Not that it mattered, Josephine said, because the last time she had seen him, nothing came of it, anyhow. So that was that. Because she was not a one to beg—she had some money of her own and livestock as well. As far as that was concerned, she had some woolen blankets, and two beds complete with bedding, too, nor did she lack clothes: she had many changes, both underthings and top ones. Yet in spite of that she had started some more weaving.

I asked in some surprise whether they had been engaged. I had had no inkling—

No, but—. Well, not exactly engaged with a ring, and plighting the troth and all. But that had been their intention. Because otherwise why should that schoolmistress, that sister of his, Sophie Palm, have come up and stayed for nothing at the Tore Peak farm for two whole summers, and behaved as though she were a lady? No, thank you, that was the end of that. Anyhow, that was what she, Josephine, had thought once, but it was a Providence that it wasn't going to happen, because there would never have been anything but trouble. So it was just as well.

Suddenly Josephine caught herself up:

"Good gracious—I nearly forgot to buy the indigo. It's for my weaving. Lucky I remembered it! Well—thanks for your hospitality."

XXXIV

It was between Christmas and the New Year, and I had accompanied Nikolai to his home. Since the town workshop was closed in any case, he had decided to go home and fell timber in the woods.

It was a big farmhouse, enlarged from the old cottage by Nikolai's father, while Nikolai himself had moved up the roof and built on a second story. He has plenty of room for me; I have a small room to myself.

His mother is hard-working and honest; she has a few animals to see to, and usually she is washing something or other, even if it is nothing more than some empty potato sacks. She cooks on the kitchen stove, and keeps her pots and pans shining. She is cleanly, and strains her milk through a muslin cloth, which she afterward washes and rinses twice. But she picks food remnants from between the prongs of forks with a hairpin!

A mirror, pictures of the German Kaiser's family, and a crucifix hang on the walls of the living room; in one corner are two shelves with oddments, including a hymnbook and a book of sermons. They are still simple and orthodox in these parts. The rest of the furniture in the house, the chairs and tables and cupboards and a cleverly constructed chest, have all been made by Nikolai himself.

Nikolai is just as slow and speechless here as in the town; the day after we arrived he went out to the woods without telling his mother. When I asked for him, she said:

"I saw him take the sleigh, so I expect he's gone to the woods."

His mother's name is Petra, and judging from her appearance she cannot be much over forty; like her son, she is ruddy and big-muscled, with a fair complexion and thick, graying hair, a veritable lion's mane. Her eyes are good companions to her hair—dark, and a little worn now, but still good enough to see far and sharply across the fjord. She, too, is taciturn, like all the peasants here, and usually keeps her large mouth shut.

I ask her how long she has been a widow, and she says, "For nearly a generation—no, don't let me tell a lie," she corrects herself. "Sophie is four and twenty now, and it was the year after her birth that he died."

They had only been married a couple of years. Nikolai is six and twenty.

I ponder over this arithmetic, but as I am old and incapable, I cannot make it tally.

Petra was very proud of her children, especially Sophie, who had gone to school and passed an examination, and now held such an important post. Of course her inheritance was used up, but she had her learning instead. Nobody could ever take that from her. A big, handsome girl, Sophie—look, here is her portrait.

I said I had met her at Tore Peak.

At Tore Peak? Oh, yes, she spent her summers there so as to be among her equals; you couldn't blame her for that. But she came home every year, too, as sure as the year came round itself. So I had met her at Tore Peak?

Sometimes I went with Nikolai to the forest for timber, and made myself slightly useful. He is as strong as an ox, and has endurance almost to the point of insensibility—a cut, black eye—nothing. And now it becomes evident that his brain works well, too. He should have had a horse, yes, but he cannot keep a horse till he can provide more fodder. But he cannot buy more pasture land till he has more money. But he was learning more about his trade in the town, and when he had finished his course of training, he would earn more money. After that he would buy a horse.

I visited the neighbors, too. The farms were small, but the farmers cultivated as much land as they required, and there was no poverty. Here were no flowerpots in the windows or pictures on the walls, as at Petra's; but good, thick furs with woven backs hung over the doors, and the children looked healthy and well-fed. The neighbors all knew I lived at Petra's house; every visitor to this district lived at Petra's house—had done so as long as they could remember. I could sense no hostility to Petra in these silent people, but the old schoolmaster was more talkative, and he was quite ready to spread gossip about her. This man was a bachelor; he had his own house and did his own housework. Had he, perhaps, at some time felt a secret desire for the widow Petra?

The schoolmaster gossiped thus:

People who had visited the village in Petra's girlhood always used to live at her parents' house. There was a room and a loft, and the engineer that planned the big road lived there, and so did the two traveling preachers, to say nothing of the itinerant peddlers who toured the district all the year round. So it went on for many a year, with the children growing up, and Petra getting big and hearty. Then Palm came; he was a Swede, a big merchant—a wholesale merchant, one might almost say, for that period, with his own boat and even a boy to carry his wares. Well, there were glass panes again in the windows of Petra's parents' house, and there was meat on Sundays, for Palm liked things done in style. He gave Petra presents of dress materials and sweets. Then he was finished with Petra, and went away to do business elsewhere. But it happened that the child Petra gave birth to was a boy, and when Palm returned and saw him, he stayed, and traveled no more. They married, and Palm added two rooms to the house, for it was his intention to open a shop there. But when he had built honestly and well, he died. His widow was left with two small children, but she had means enough, for Palm had had plenty of money. Then why did not Petra remarry? She could have got a man in spite of the handicap of two small children, for Petra herself was still a young girl. But from her childhood days, said the schoolmaster, she had been spoiled by this love of roving company, and again housed itinerant tramps and Swedes and peddlers, and thoroughly disgraced herself. Some of them stayed there for weeks, eating and drinking and idling. It was shameful. Her parents saw nothing wrong in this because it had always been their way of living, and besides it brought them a little money. So the years went by. When the children were grown and Sophie was out of the way, she might have married even then, for she still had half her money left, and being childless again, it was not too late. But no, Petra didn't want to, and it was too late, she said; it was the children's turn to marry now, she said.

"Well, she's pretty old now, isn't she?" I said.

"Yes, time passes," the schoolmaster replied. "I don't know whether anyone has asked her this year, but last year there was someone—one person—or so I've heard, so I've been told. But Petra didn't want to. If I could only guess what she's waiting for."

"Perhaps she's not waiting at all."

"Well, it's all the same to me," says the schoolmaster. "But she takes in all these tramps and peddlers and carries on and makes a public nuisance of herself...."

As I walked home from the schoolmaster's, I found I understood Petra's arithmetic much better.

Nikolai has gone back to his workshop in the town, but I have remained behind. It matters little where I am, for the winter makes a dead man of me in any case.

To pass the time, I carefully measure the piece of land that Nikolai is going to break up when he can afford it, and I calculate what it will cost him, with drainage and everything: a bare two hundred kroner. Then he could keep a horse. It would have been an act of charity to give him this money in case his mother could not. He could have added another field to his land then.

138

"Look here, Petra—why don't you give Nikolai the two hundred kroner he needs for fodder for a horse?"

"And four hundred to buy the horse," she muttered.

"That makes six."

"I haven't got such a lot of six hundred kroners lying about."

"But wouldn't the horse be useful for plowing?"

A pause. Then:

"He can break the ground himself."

I was not unfamiliar with this line of reasoning. Everyone has his own problems, and Petra had hers. But the strange thing is that each one of us struggles for himself as though he had a hundred years to live. I once knew two brothers named Martinsen who owned a large farm, the produce of which they sold. Both were well-to-do bachelors without heirs. But both had diseased lungs, the younger brother's much worse than the elder's. In the spring, the younger brother became permanently bedridden, but though he approached his end, he still maintained an interest in everything that went on at the farm. He heard strangers talking in the kitchen and called his brother in.

"What is it?" he asked.

"Only someone to buy eggs."

"What's the price per score now?"

His brother told him.

"Then give him the small eggs," he cautioned.

A few days later he was dead. His brother lived till his sixty-seventh year, though his lungs were diseased. When anybody came to buy eggs, he always gave him the smallest....

"But," I insisted to Petra, "Nikolai doesn't want to waste time breaking his ground himself, does he? Surely if he works at his trade he'll earn more!"

"They don't pay for joinery here," Petra replied. "People buy their chairs and tables from the shops now; it's cheaper."

"Then why is Nikolai working as an apprentice?"

"I've asked him the same question," she replied. "Nikolai just wants to be a carpenter, but it won't get him anywhere. Still, he can do as he likes."

"Well, what else could he do?"

A pause. Petra's big mouth is closed. But at length she says:

"There's plenty of traffic now and a lot of tourists in the summer, both at Tore Peak and down here on the headland. One time we had two Danes living here; they had traveled on foot. 'If you had a horse, you could have driven us here,' they said to me."

"Ah," I thought to myself, "the cat sticking its nose out of the bag!"

"'You've got a big house and four rooms,' the Danes said, and 'There are high mountains and big woods,' they said, 'and fish in the fjord and fish in the river; there are lots of things here, and there's a broad road here,' they said. Nikolai was standing next to them and heard it all, too. 'Now we're here,' they said, 'but we can't get away again unless we walk.'"

Just to say something, I asked her:

"Four rooms—I thought you only had three?"

"Yes, but the workshop could be turned into a room, too," the big mouth replied.

"So that's it!" I thought. With hardly a pause, I continued:

"But if Nikolai were going to deal with tourists, he'd have to get a horse, wouldn't he?"

"Well, I suppose we could have managed it," Petra replied.

"It's four hundred kroner."

"Yes," she said, "and the carriage a hundred and fifty."

"But this land won't feed a horse!"

"What do other people feed horses on?" she asked. "They buy sacks of oats on the headland."

"That's eighteen kroner a sack."

"No, seventeen. And you earn as much as that on your first tourist."

Yes, Petra had it all figured out; she was the born landlady, and had grown up in a lodginghouse. She could cook, too, for had she not put two snakes of Italian macaroni in the barley broth? The money for coffee, for the bed at night and waffles in the morning, had grown so dear to her that she hid it away, watched it increase, and grew rich on it. She did not produce like other peasant women, but no one can do everything at one time, and Petra was a parasite. She did not want to live by earning something; she wanted to live on the tourists who earned enough themselves, and could afford to come.

Splendor and Englishmen, no doubt, in these parts! If it all works out as it should—and it probably will.

It is February. I have an idea, a vagrant idea that comes to me, and I harbor it: now that there is a little snow, and its crust is hard, I shall walk across the fields into Sweden. That is what I shall do.

But before I can do it, I must wait for my laundry, and Petra, who is cleanly, washes in many waters. So I pass the time in Nikolai's workshop, where there are many kinds of planes and saws and drills and lathes, and there I fashion strange things. For the small boys of the neighboring farm, I make a windmill that will really turn in the wind. It whirls and rattles well, and I remember my own childhood when we called this apparatus onomatopoeically a windwhirr.

Besides this, I go out walking, and use my winter head as well as I can, which is not very well. I do not blame the winter, nor do I blame anything. But where are the red-hot irons and the youth of omnipotence? For hours sometimes I walk along a path in the woods with my hands folded on my back, an old man, my mind gilded for a moment by an occasional memory; I stop, and raise my eyebrows in surprise. Can this be an iron in the fire? It is not, for it fades again, and I am left behind in a quiet melancholy.

But in order to recall my young days, I pretend to be filled with a heaven-sent energy. It is by no means all pretense, and pictures rise in my mind, fragmentary flageolet tones:

> We came from the meadow
> and downy heather;
> we came from friendship,
> too-loo-loo-lay!
> A star that watched
> saw lips meet lips.

141

None else so dear,
so sweet as you.

Those youthful days,
those happy days,
unmatched since then!
but what am I now?
The bees once swarmed,
the swan once played.
There's no play now,
yet too-loo-loo-lay!

I break off, and put the pencil in my pocket with a tone still resounding within me. I walk on with some pleasure to myself, at least.

There is a letter for me. Who on earth has found me out here? The letter is as follows:

Forgive me for writing you, but I should like to talk to you about something that has happened. I should like to see you as soon as you come back. There's nothing the matter. Please don't say no.

Yours,

Ingeborg Torsen

I reread it many times. "Something that has happened." But I'm going to Sweden, I'm going to move about a little, and stop losing myself in the affairs of others. Do they think I am mankind's old uncle, that I can be summoned hither and thither to give advice? Excuse me, but I am going to assert myself and become quite inaccessible; the snow is just right, and I have planned a big journey—a business tour, I might almost call it, very important to me—I have a great deal at stake.... How composite is the mind of man! As I sit talking drivel to myself, and even sometimes saying an angry word aloud in order that Petra may hear it, I am not at all displeased at having received this letter; in fact secretly I am so pleased that I feel ashamed. It is merely because I shall soon see the town again—the town with its frostbitten gardens and its ships.

But what on earth can this mean? Has she been to my landlady's and got my address? Or has she met Nikolai?

I left at once.

XXXV

My landlady was surprised.

"Why, good evening. How well and happy you look! Here's your mail."

"Let it lie. I must tell you, Madame Henriksen, that you are a jewel."

"Ha, ha, ha!"

"Yes, you are. You are a very kind woman. But you have given my address to someone."

"No, indeed; I swear I haven't."

"No? Well, then someone else must have done so. Yes, you're right, I am happy, and tomorrow morning I shall get up very early and walk down by the shore."

"But I did send a message," said my landlady. "I hope it wasn't wrong of me. To a lady who wanted to know as soon as you arrived."

"A lady? You sent a message just now?"

"A little while ago, as soon as you came in. A young, handsome lady; she might have been your daughter, you know."

"Thank you."

"Well, I'm only saying what's so. She said she would come at once, because she had to see you about something."

The landlady left me.

So Miss Torsen was coming this very evening; something must have happened. She had never visited me before. I looked round; yes, everything was neat and tidy. I washed and made myself ready. There, she can have that chair; I'd better light the other lamp, too. It might not be a bad idea to sit down to my correspondence; that would make a good impression, and if I put some letters in a small, feminine hand on top, it might even make her a little jealous—hee, hee. Oh, God, ten or fifteen years ago one could play such tricks; it's too late now....

143

Then she knocked and came in.

I made no move to shake hands, and neither did she; I merely drew out a chair for her.

"Excuse my coming like this," she said. "I asked Mrs. Henriksen to send me a message; it's nothing serious, and now I feel a little embarrassed about it, but—"

I saw that it was something serious, and my heart began to pound. Why should my heart be affected?

"This is the first time you've been in my rooms," I said, expectant and on the defensive.

"Yes. It's very nice," she said, without looking round. She began to clasp her hands and pull them apart again till the tips of her gloves projected beyond her finger tips. She was in a state of great excitement.

"Perhaps now I've done something you'll approve of?" she said, suddenly pulling off her glove.

She had a ring on her finger.

"Good," I said. It didn't affect me immediately; I was to understand more later, and merely asked:

"Are you engaged?"

"Yes," she replied. And she looked at me with a smile, though her mouth shook.

I looked back at her, and I believe I said something like, "Well, now, well, well!" Then I nodded in a fatherly fashion, bowed formally, and said: "My heartiest congratulations!"

"Yes, that's what it's come to," she said. "I think it was the best thing to do. Perhaps you think it's a bit unreliable of me or rash or—well, don't you?"

"Oh, I don't know—"

"But it was absolutely the best thing. And I just thought I'd tell you."

I got up. She started, evidently in a very nervous state. But I had

144

only risen to turn down the lamp behind her, which had begun to smoke.

A pause. She said nothing more, so what could I say? But as the minutes passed and I saw she was distressed, I said:

"Why did you want to tell me this?"

"Yes—why did I?"

"Perhaps for a moment you thought you were the center of the world again, but—"

"Yes, I expect so."

She looked about her with great, roving eyes. Then she got up; she had been sitting all this time as though about to spring at me. I rose, too. An unhappy woman—I saw that plainly enough; but good heavens, what could I do? She had come to tell me she was engaged, and at the same time looked very unhappy. Was that a way to behave? But as she got up, I could see her face better under her hat—I could see her hair—the hair that was beginning to show silken and silver at the temples—how beautiful it was! She was tall and handsome, and her breast was rising and falling—her great breast—what a great breast she had, rising and falling! Her face was brown, and her mouth open, just a little open, dry, feverishly dry—

"Miss Ingeborg!"

It was the first time I called her this. And I moved my hand toward her slightly, longing to touch her, perhaps to fondle her—I don't know—

But she had collected herself now, and stood erect and hard. Her eyes had grown cold; they looked at me, putting me in my place again, as she walked toward the door. A cry of "No!" escaped me.

"What's the matter?" she asked.

"Don't go, not yet, not at once; sit down again and talk to me more."

"No, you're quite right," she said. "I'm not the center of the universe. Here I come to bother you with my unimportant troubles, and you— well, of course, you're busy with your extensive correspondence."

"Look here, sit down again, won't you? I shan't even read the letters;

they're nothing, only two or three letters perhaps, probably from complete strangers. Now sit down; tell me everything; you owe me that much. Look, I shan't even read the letters."

And with that I swept them up and threw them into the fire.

"Oh—what are you doing?" she cried, and ran to the fireplace, trying to save them.

"Don't bother," I said. "I expect no happiness to come to me through the post, and sorrows I do not seek."

She stood so close to me that I found myself again on the point of touching her, just for a moment, touching her arm; but I caught myself in time. I had already gone too far, so I said as gently and sympathetically as I could:

"Dear child, you must not be unhappy; it will all turn out for the best; you'll see. Now sit down—there, that's better."

No doubt she had been taken aback by my violence, for she sank into her chair almost absently.

"I'm not unhappy," she said.

"Aren't you? So much the better!"

I began to chatter away at top speed, though I tried to restrain myself, to show that I was nothing more than an uncle to her. I talked to distract her, to distract us both; I let my tongue wag—I could hear it buzzing. What could I say? A little of everything—a great deal, in fact:

"Well, well, child. And whom are you marrying, who is the lucky man? Nice of you to come and tell me before anyone, really very nice; thank you very much. You see I've only just come home and I haven't slept much on the journey. I was anxious to know—well, perhaps not anxious exactly—but still—You know what such a homecoming is: lots of people, noise, brr!—I hardly got any sleep. Then I came home, and then you came along—thank you for coming, Miss Ingeborg—I might be your father and you're just a child; that's why I say 'Ingeborg.' But when you told me all this, I hadn't had any sleep, I wasn't quite balanced—not enough to give you advice; I mean, I hadn't quite appreciated—But now you can quite safely—I'd like to know, of course—Is he old? Is he young? Young, of course. I am imagining what will happen to you now, Miss

Ingeborg, in your new condition. I mean, it will be so entirely different from what you've been accustomed to, but God bless you, it will all turn out for the best, I'm sure of that—"

"But you don't even know who it is!" she interrupted, looking at me apprehensively again.

"No, I don't, and I needn't if you'd rather not tell me yet. Who is it? A dapper little man, I can see that from his ring, a schoolmaster perhaps, a clever young schoolmaster—"

She shook her head.

"Then a big, good-natured man who wants to dance with you—"

"Yes, perhaps," she said slowly.

"There you are—you see I've guessed it. A bear who will carry you on his paws. On your birthday—do you know what he'll give you for your birthday?"

But perhaps I was getting too childish; I bored her, and for the first time she looked away from me, looked at a picture on the wall, then at another picture. But it was not easy for me to stop now, after having spoken hardly at all for several weeks, and feeling profoundly excited besides—heaven only knows why.

"How did you like the country?" she asked suddenly. As I could not see the drift of this question, I merely looked at her.

"Weren't you at Nikolai's mother's house?" she persisted.

"Yes."

"What is she like?"

"Are you interested in her?"

"No, I don't suppose so. Oh dear!" she sighed wearily.

"Come, come, you mustn't sound like that when you're newly engaged! What the country was like? Well, there was a schoolmaster—you know, an old bachelor, sly, and amusing. Said he knew me, and put on the most extraordinary airs the first day. And of course I returned the compliment and said I had come exclusively to meet him. 'Impossible!' he said. 'Why should it be?' I said; 'forty

147

years a schoolmaster, a respected man, permanent churchman, chairman, indispensable everywhere!' Well, then I attended his class. Most impressive. He talked continually; for once he had an audience, almost like a school inspection. 'You there, Peter! Ahem,' he said. 'There was a horse and a man, and one of them was riding on the other's back. Which one was riding, Peter?' 'The man,' Peter replies. A pause. 'Well, maybe you're right, Peter—maybe the man was riding. Just like sin, like the devil riding us....'"

But she was looking at the wall again, drifting away from me again. I changed the subject clumsily:

"Of course you'd rather hear about people you know—about Tore Peak, for instance. Josephine has been in town."

"Yes, I know," she said, nodding her head.

"Remember the old man at Tore Peak? I don't think I'll ever forget him. In a certain number of years I shall be like him—perhaps not quite so old. Then I shall be a child again with age. One day he came out, and went down to the field. I saw him; he had mittens on. You know he eats all sorts of things, and I saw him lie down and eat the hay."

She stared at me foolishly.

"But I must say he didn't look as though he had ever eaten hay before—possibly because it was rotting. It was the hay that had been left, you know—rotting down for next year—for the next tourist year."

"You seem to think," she said smiling, "that you have to cheer me up, because I'm terribly unhappy. I'm quite the reverse. Perhaps he's too good for me; that's what his sister seems to think, anyhow, because she tried to stop it. But I'm going to enjoy snubbing that sister of his. Anyhow, I'm not unhappy, and that isn't the reason I've come. I'd really much rather have him than anyone else—since I can't get the one I really want."

"You've told me this before, child—last winter, in fact. But the man you want has gone his way—besides, you said yourself that you didn't belong with him, or rather, that he didn't with you—I mean-"

"Belong? Do I belong anywhere? Do you think I belong in the place I'm going to now? I'm afraid I'm not really suitable for anybody—at least I can't think of anyone I'd suit. I wonder how I'll manage. I wonder if he'll be able to stand me. But I'll do my very best; I've made up my mind to that."

"Well, who is it—do I know him? Of course you suit each other. I can't believe you don't. He must be in love with you, quite madly in love, and you must love him in return. I'm sure you'll come through with flying colors, Miss Ingeborg, because you're capable and intelligent."

"Oh, well," she said, rising suddenly to her feet. But she hesitated over something, and seemed about to speak, then changed her mind again. At the door, she stood with her back to me, pulling on her gloves, and said:

"So you think I ought to do it?"

I was taken aback by the question, and replied:

"Ought to do it? Haven't you done it already?"

"Yes. That is—well, yes, I've done it, I'm engaged. And I can tell from your manner that I've done the right thing."

"Well, I don't know. I can't tell."

I crossed the room to her.

"Who is it?"

"Oh, God, no; let's drop it. I can't bear any more now. Good night."

She stretched her hand out fumblingly, but since she was looking at the floor, she could not find mine, and both our hands circled helplessly round each other for a moment. Then she opened the door and was gone. I called to her, begging her to wait, seized my hat, and hurried after her. An empty staircase. I rushed down and opened the street door. An empty street. She must have run.

"I'll try to see her tomorrow," I thought.

One day, two days, but I did not see her, though I went to all the usual places. Another day—nothing. Then I thought I would go up to her home and inquire about her. At first this did not seem to me too improper, but when it came to the point, I hesitated. There is, after all, something to be lost by making a fool of oneself. But was I not a kind of uncle? No—yes, of course, but still—

149

A week passes, two weeks, three. The girl has quite disappeared; I hope she hasn't had an accident. I mount the stairs to her home and ring the bell....

She's already gone away; they left as soon as they were married, last week. She's married to Nikolai, Carpenter Nikolai.

March—what a month! The winter is over, yet there's no telling how much longer it may still last. That's what March is for.

I have lived through another winter and seen the nigger entertainment at the Anglo-Saxon theater. You were there too, my friend. You saw how cleverly we all turned somersaults. Why, you even took part yourself, and you carry about a broken rib as a cherished little memento of the occasion. I saw it all from a slight distance away, ten miles, to be exact; no people were near me, but there were seven heavens above.

And pretty soon I shall be reading what the officials have to say about the year's harvest in our country; that is to say, the harvest at the theater—in dollars, and in sterling.

The waggish professor is enjoying himself, quite in his element. There he goes, self-assured and complacent, Sir Mediocrity in all his glory. By next year, he will have dragged other progressive people in his wake; he will have dressed up Norway still more, and made it still more attractive to the Anglo-Saxons. More dollars, and more sterling.

What, do I hear someone objecting?

Yes, Switzerland.

Well, then, we shall invite Switzerland to dinner and toast her thus: "Colleague, our great aim is to resemble you. Who else can squeeze so much profit out of their mountains? Who else can file at such clockwork? Switzerland, make yourself at home; we don't want to rob you; there are no pickpockets at this table. Here's to you!"

But if that doesn't help, we shall have to roll up our sleeves and fight. There are still Norwegians left in good old Norway, and our rival—is Switzerland.

Mrs. Henriksen brings catkins in a vase into my room.

"What, is it spring?"

"Oh, it's getting on."

"Then I shall be going away. You see, Mrs. Henriksen, I should very much have liked to stay, because this is really where I belong; but what more can I do here? I don't work; I merely idle. Do you understand me? I grieve continually, and my heart sits wrinkled. My most brilliant achievement is spinning coins: I toss a coin into the air and wait. When I came here last autumn I wasn't so bad, not nearly so bad. I was only half a year younger then, yet I was ten years younger. What has happened to me since? Nothing. Only—I'm not a better man than I was last autumn."

"But you've been all right all winter, haven't you? And three weeks ago, when you came back from the country, you were so happy!"

"Was I? I don't remember that. Ah, well, things don't move so fast, and nothing has happened to me in these three weeks. Well, never mind; at all events, I shall go away. I must travel when the spring comes. I have always done so in the past, and I want to do the same thing now. Sit down, Mrs. Henriksen."

"No, thank you, I'm too busy."

Too busy! Yes, you work—you're not ten years older than you were last autumn. You think it's hard work to rest on Sundays, don't you? Dear Madame Henriksen! You and your little daughter knit stockings for the whole family, you let your rooms, you keep your family together like a mother. But you mustn't let your little Louise sit for twelve years on a school form. If you do, you'll hardly ever see her all through her youth, those formative years of her life. And then she can't be like you or learn from you. She'll learn to have children easily enough, but she won't learn to be a mother, and when the time comes for her to keep her home and family together, she will not be able to do it. She'll only know "languages" and mathematics and the story of Bluebeard, but that is not food for the heart of a woman. That is twelve years of continual famine for her soul.

"Excuse my asking, but where are you going to?"

"I don't know, but I'm going. Why, where should I go? I shall go aboard a steamship and sail, and when I have sailed long enough, I will go ashore. If I find, on looking about me, that I have traveled too far or not far enough, I shall board a ship again and sail on. Once I walked across into Sweden as far as Kalmar and even Öland, but that was too far, so I turned back. No one cares to know where I am, least of all myself."

XXXVI

You get used to everything; you even get used to the passage of two years.

And now it is spring again....

It is market day in the frontier town; my room is noisy, for there is music down in the fields, the roundabout is whirling, the tightrope walker is gossiping outside his tent, and people of every sort throng the village. The crowds are great, and there is even a sprinkling of Norwegians from across the border. Horses snort and whinny, cows low, and trading is brisk.

In the display window of the goldsmith across the road, a great cow of silver has made its appearance, a handsome breeder that the local farmers stop to admire.

"She's too smart for my crags," says one of them with a laugh.

"What do you think's her price?" says another with a laugh.

"Why, do you want to buy her?"

"No, haven't got fodder enough this year."

A man trudges placidly down the road and also stops in front of this window. I see him from behind, and take note of his massive back. He stands there a long time, trying to make up his mind, no doubt, for now and then he scratches his beard. There he goes, sure enough, entering the shop with a ponderous tread. I wonder if he intends to buy the silver cow!

It takes him an age, and still he hasn't come out. What on earth is he doing in there? Now that I have begun to watch him, I might as well go the whole hog. So I put on my hat and cross to the goldsmith's window myself, mingling with the other spectators, and watching the door.

At last the man re-emerges—yes, it is Nikolai. It was his back and hands, but he has got a beard now, too. He looks splendid. Imagine Carpenter Nikolai being here!

We greet each other, and we talk as he shakes me slowly and

ponderously by the hand. Our conversation is halting, but we get on. Yes, of course, he has gone into the shop on business, in a kind of way.

"You've not bought the silver cow, have you?"

"Oh, no, not that. It didn't amount to anything, really. In fact, I didn't buy anything."

By degrees, I discover that he is buying a horse. And he tells me that he has dug that piece of land of his, and is turning it into pasture, and his wife—oh, yes, thank you for asking—she lives in health to this day.

"By the way," he said, "have you come here over the fjeld?"

"Yes, I came last winter. In December."

"What a pity I didn't know!"

I explained that I hadn't had the time to visit his home then; I was in a hurry, there was some business—

"Yes, I understand," he said.

We said little more, for Nikolai was as taciturn as ever. Besides, he had other business to attend to; he cannot absent himself from the farm for long, and had to return next day.

"Have you bought your horse yet?"

"Well, no, I haven't."

"Do you think you will?"

"I don't know yet. I'm trying to split a difference of five and twenty kroner."

Later I saw Nikolai going to the goldsmith's again. He seemed to do a great deal of business there.

"I could have company across the fjeld now," I thought. "It's spring, and do I not always travel in the spring?"

I began to pack my knapsack.

Nikolai emerged once more, apparently as empty-handed as he had entered. I opened my window and called to him to ask if he had bought the horse.

"N-no—the man won't meet my price."

"Well, can't you meet his?"

"Y-yes, I could," he replied slowly. "But I don't think I've got enough money on me."

"I could lend you some."

At this Nikolai smiled and shook his head as though my offer were a fairy tale.

"Thank you just the same," he said, turning to walk away.

"Where are you going now?" I asked.

"To look at another horse. It's old and small, still—"

Was I thrusting myself on the man? I? Nonsense! I don't see that at all. He felt offended because I had passed his door last winter without stopping and now I wanted to make him friendly again. That was all. But as I wanted no cause for self-reproach, I stopped packing, nor would I ask Nikolai if I might go back with him. But I went out for a walk in the town. I had as much right to do that as anyone.

I met Nikolai in the street with a colt, and we stopped to exchange a few words.

"Is it yours?"

"Yes, I've bought her; the man met me halfway after all," he replied with a smile.

We walked along to the stable together and fed and petted the horse. She was a mare, two and a half years old, with a tawny coat and an off-white mane and tail—a perfect little lady.

That evening Nikolai came over to my room of his own accord for a chat about the mare and the state of the roads. When he was saying good-bye at the door, he seemed struck by a sudden thought.

"By the way," he said, "I suppose it's no good asking you, but you

154

could get a lift for your knapsack, you know. We could be there day after tomorrow," he added.

How could I offend him again?

We walked all next day, spent the night in the mountain hut at the frontier, and then went on again. Nikolai carried my knapsack all the way, as well as his own smaller parcels. When I suggested that we should share the burden, he said it was no weight at all. I think Nikolai wanted to spare the little tawny lady.

At noon we saw the fjord beneath us. Nikolai stopped and carefully rubbed down the mare once more. As our path sloped downward, I felt a pressure, a contraction in my chest; it was the sea air. Nikolai asked me what was the matter, but it was nothing.

On reaching his home, we found the yard well swept, and in the doorway a woman on her knees with her back toward us, scrubbing the floor. It was the Saturday cleaning day.

"Hullo!" Nikolai roared in a tremendously loud voice, stopping dead in his tracks as he did so.

The woman in the doorway looked round; her hair was gray, but it was she, Miss Ingeborg, Fru[1] Ingeborg.

"Good heavens!" she exclaimed, hastily mopping up the rest of the floor.

"Look at all the cleaning that goes on here!" Nikolai said, laughing. "That's her idea of fun!"

And I had believed Carpenter Nikolai incapable of lightheartedness! Yet I had seen how content he had been all the way home, how deeply content, and proud of the little lady he was bringing with him. Even now he was still stroking her.

Fru Ingeborg rose to her feet, her skirts dark with the damp. It all seemed strange to me; her hair was so gray. I needed a little time, a moment, to collect myself, and turned away to give her time, too.

"What a lovely horse!" I heard her exclaim.

Nikolai went on stroking the mare.

---

[1] Mrs. (Translator's note.)

"I've brought a visitor with me," he said.

I went to her and perhaps—I don't know—perhaps I rather overdid my unconcern. I greeted her and insisted on shaking her wet hand, which she hesitated to give me. I was anxious to appear quite formal with her, and shook her hand as I repeated my greeting.

"Well, of all people!" she replied.

I persisted in my formal attitude.

"You must blame your husband," I said. "It's his fault that I'm here."

"I wish you heartily welcome," she returned. "How lucky I've just got through the cleaning!"

A slight pause. We looked at each other; two years had passed since our last meeting. To break the silence, we all began to admire the mare, Nikolai swelling with pride. Then we heard a child calling from within the house, and the young mother ran off.

"Come in, won't you!" she called back over her shoulder.

As soon as I entered, I saw that the room had been changed. There was too much middle-class frippery: white curtains at the windows, numerous pictures on the walls, a lamp pendent from the ceiling, underneath it in the center of the room a round table and chairs, knickknacks in a china cupboard, a pink-painted spinning wheel, flowers in pots—in short, the room was crowded. This, no doubt, was the sort of thing Fru Ingeborg had been used to and considered in good taste. But in Petra's day, this had been a light and spacious room.

"How's your mother?" I asked Nikolai.

As usual he was slow to reply. His wife answered for him:

"She's very well."

I wanted to ask, "Where is she?" but I refrained.

"Look, I want to show you something," said Fru Ingeborg.

It was the child in his bed—a boy, big and handsome, about a year old. He frowned at me at first, but only for a moment. As soon as he was on his mother's arm, he looked at me without fear.

How happy and beautiful the young mother looked! Peerless, indeed, with her eyes full of an inscrutable graciousness she had not possessed before.

"What a fine little man!" I said, admiring the boy.

"I should think he was!" said the mother.

You get used to everything. The sea air no longer oppresses me; I can speak without losing my breath to the woman who is now the mistress of this house. She likes to talk, too, pouring out her words nervously, as though it had been a long time since she last opened her mouth. What we talked about? Well, we neither asked nor answered questions about measuring angles or analyzing Shakespeare's grammar.

Had she ever thought her matriculation would land her up here, amid livestock and Saturday cleaning?

Oh, that parody of an education! She had taken the first toddling steps in a dozen sciences, but if she met someone with fully adult knowledge she was lost. She had other things to think about now, her home and her family and the farm. Of course there wasn't much livestock, now that Nikolai's mother had taken half of it with her—

"Has Petra gone away?"

Married—to the schoolmaster. No, Petra hadn't wanted to stay when the young wife took possession. One evening a strange man had come to the house, and Petra had wanted to admit him, but Fru Ingeborg would not. She knew who he was and wanted him to leave. So there were quarrels between the older woman and the young one.

Petra was also dissatisfied with the young wife's work in the barn. It was true she was not very skillful, but she was learning all the time, and enjoyed improving her skill. She never asked questions; that, she saw, would have been foolish, but she worked things out by herself, and kept her eyes open when she visited neighboring farms. That didn't mean to say she could learn everything. There were things she never learned properly because she was not "to the manner born." Often the wives of rural officials are from small towns, and have not learned the ways of the country, though they must learn them in time. But they never learn them well. They know only just enough for their daily needs. To set up a weave, you must

157

have grown up with the sound of the shuttle in your ears; to tend the cattle as they should be tended, you must have helped your mother since childhood. You can learn from others, but it will not be in your blood.

Not everyone has a man like Nikolai to live with, either. The young wife is very fond of her Nikolai, this sound, hearty bear who loves her in return. Besides, Nikolai is not exacting; his wife seems to him peerless in all she does. Of course she has taken great pains; it has left its mark on her, too, and she is not gray for nothing. A few months ago she lost a front tooth, too—broke it on some bird shot left in the breast of a ptarmigan she was eating. She hardly dared look in the mirror now—didn't recognize herself. But what did it matter as long as Nikolai....

Look what he'd brought her, this brooch, bought at the goldsmith's at the market: wasn't it lovely? Oh, Nikolai was mad; but she would do anything in the world for him, too. Imagine using some of the money for the horse on a brooch! Where is he now, where's he gone to? She'll bet anything he's stroking the mare again.

"Nikolai!" she called.

"Yes," his reply came from the stable.

She sat down again, crossing her legs. Her face had turned pink; perhaps a thought, a memory, passed through her mind. She was suffused with excitement and beauty. Her dress clung to her body, outlining its contours. She began gently to stroke her knee.

"Is the child asleep?" I asked. I had to say something.

"Yes, he's asleep. And think of him!" she exclaimed. "Can you imagine anything more wonderful? Excuse my talking like this, but.... You know he's not a year old yet. I never knew children were such a blessing."

"Well, you see they are."

"Yes, I thought differently once; I remember that perfectly well, and you contradicted me. Of course it was stupid of me. Children? Miracles! And when you're old, they're the only happiness—the last happiness. I shall have more; I shall have many of them, a whole row of them, like organ pipes, each taller than the last. They're lovely.... But I wish I hadn't lost my tooth; it leaves such a black gap.

I really feel quite bad about it, on Nikolai's account. I suppose a false one could be put in, but I shouldn't dream of it. Besides, I understand it's quite dear. But I've given up using any arts; I only wish I'd stopped earlier—I've gone on much too long. Think of all I've missed by it: all my childhood, all my youth. Haven't I idled away whole summers at resorts, even as a grown woman? I needed a holiday from my school work, a rest, and immediately turned it into sheer futility, every day a disgrace. I could cry with regret. I should have been married ten years ago, and had my husband all that time, and a home and many children. Now I'm already old, cheated out of ten years of my life, with gray hair and one tooth gone—"

"Well, you've lost one tooth, but I've hardly got one left!"

No sooner had I consoled her thus than I regretted it. Why should I make myself worse than I am? Things were bad enough anyhow. I was sick with fury at myself, and grinned and grimaced to show her my teeth: "Here, don't miss them, have a good look!" But I'm afraid she saw what a fool I was making of myself; everything I did was wrong.

Then she consoled me in her turn, as people do when they can well afford it:

"What, you old? Nonsense!"

"Have you met the schoolmaster?" I asked abruptly.

"Of course. I remember what you told me about him: a horse and a man came riding along the road.... But he's got sense, and he's terribly stingy. Oh, he's cunning; he borrows our harrow because ours is new and good. They've built a house at the end of the valley, and take in travelers—quite a big hotel, in fact, with the waitresses dressed in national costume. Of course Nikolai and I both went to the wedding; Petra really looked a charming and lovely bride. You mustn't think she and I are still unfriendly; she likes me better now that I'm more competent, and last summer they sent for me several times to interpret for some English people and that sort of thing—at least I know how to say soap and food and conveyance and tips in other languages!

"But I don't think I should ever have had any serious trouble with Petra in the first place if Sophie hadn't come home—you know, the schoolmistress in the town. She's always found plenty to criticize in me, so I never liked her very much, I must admit. But when she came here, she was very arrogant toward me, and lorded it over me, showing off all her knowledge. I was busy trying to learn what I needed to know for the life up here, and then she came along and made me look small, talking about the Seven Years' War all the time. She was terribly learned about the Seven Years' War, because that's what she had in her examination. And our way of talking wasn't elegant enough for her; Nikolai used rough country expressions sometimes, and she didn't like that. But Nikolai speaks quite well enough, and I can't see what that fool of a sister of his has got to put on airs for! And on top of that she came home to stay—for six months, anyhow. She'd been engaged, so then she had to take a six months' holiday. The baby's with Petra, with his grandmother, so he's well taken care of. It's a boy, too, but he's hardly got any hair; mine has plenty of hair. Well, in a way, of course, it's a pity about Sophie, because she'd used up her legacy and her youth studying to be a schoolmistress, and then she comes home like that. But she really was insufferable, thinking she was a lot better than I because she hadn't been discharged, like me. So I asked her to leave. And then they both left, Sophie and her mother. Anyhow, her mother and I are quite reconciled.

"But you mustn't think we've had any help from her to buy the horse. Nothing of the kind! We borrowed the money from the bank. But we'll manage, because it's our only debt. Nikolai has made all the furniture in here himself, the table and china cupboard and everything; we haven't bought a thing. He's dug up the new field himself, too. And we'll be getting more cattle; you ought to see what a handsome heifer we've got....

"Even the food wasn't good enough for Sophie. Tins saved such a lot of trouble, she said; we ought to buy tinned food. It was enough to make you sick to listen to her. I was just beginning to knit, too; I'd got one of my neighbors to teach me, and I was knitting stockings for myself. But of course Lady Sophie—well, she bought her stockings in the city. Oh, she was charming. 'Get out!' I said to her. So they left."

Nikolai entered the room.

"Did you want me?"

"No—oh, yes, I wanted you to come upstairs with me. I need something to hang things on in front of the fire, a clotheshorse—come along—"

I stayed behind, thinking:

"If only it lasts, if only it lasts! She's so overwrought; living on her nerves. And pregnant again. But what splendid resolution she shows, and how she's matured in these two years! But it has cost her a great deal, too.

"Good luck to you, Ingeborg, good luck!"

At all events, she had triumphed over Schoolmistress Sophie, who had once tried so hard to set Nikolai against her. "Get out!" How content Fru Ingeborg must be—what delight in this small triumph! Life had changed so much that such things were important to her; she grew heated again when she mentioned it, and pulled at her fingers as she had done in her schooldays. And why should she not be content? A small triumph now had the rank of a bigger one in the old days. Proportions were changed, but her satisfaction was no less.

Listen—she has begun to read upstairs; there's the sound of a steady hum. Yes, it's Sunday today, and she, being the best educated of them, naturally reads the service. Bravo! Magnificent! She has extended her self-discipline even to this, for they are all orthodox Christians in this neighborhood. Believing? No, but not hostile, either. One reads Scripture. Rather a clever ruse, that of the clotheshorse.

She has become an excellent cook, too, in the peasant style. Delicious broth, without noodles, but otherwise just as it should be, with barley, carrots, and thyme. I doubt whether she has learned this at the domestic science school. I consider all the things she has learned, and find them numerous. Had she, perhaps, been a little overstrung in her talk about children like organ pipes? I don't know, but her nostrils dilated like a mare's as she spoke. She must have known how unwillingly middle-class couples have children, and how short is the love between them: in the daytime they are together so that people might not talk, but the night separates them. She was different, for she would make hers a house of fruitfulness: often she and her husband were apart during the day, when their separate labors called them, but the night united them.

Bravo, Fru Ingeborg!

XXXVII

Really, it was time I was leaving; at least I could have moved across to Petra and the Schoolmaster, who take in travelers. Really I ought to do that....

Nikolai has got his tawny lady working on the farm; she's harnessed to a neat cart that he has made himself and banded with iron. And now the lady carts manure. The tiny farm with its few head of cattle doesn't yield too much of this precious substance, so it is soon spread. Then the lady draws the plow, and looks as though it were no more than the heavy train of a ball dress behind her! Nikolai has never heard of such a horse before, and neither has his wife.

I take a walk down to the newly dug field and look at it from every angle. Then I take soil in my hand and feel it and nod, exactly as though I knew something about it. Rich, black soil—sheer perfection.

I walk so far that I can see the gargoyles on Petra's hotel—and suddenly turn off the path into the woods, to sheltered groves and catkins and peace. The air is still; spring will soon be here.

And so the days wear on.

I am comfortable and feel very much at home; how I should like to stay here! I should pay well for my keep, and make myself useful and popular; I shouldn't harm a fly. But that evening I tell Nikolai that I must think of moving on; this will not do.... And perhaps he will mention it....

"Can't you stop a while longer?" he says. "But I suppose it isn't the kind of place—"

"God bless you, Nikolai; it is the kind of place, but—well, it's spring now, and I always travel in the spring. I should have to be very low before I gave that up. And besides, I expect you're both pretty tired of me, at least your wife."

This, too, I hoped he would mention.

Then I packed my knapsack and waited. No—no one came to take the knapsack out of my hand and forbid me to pack any farther. So perhaps Nikolai hasn't mentioned it. The man never does open his mouth. So I placed the knapsack on a chair in the middle of the room, all packed and ready, for everyone to see that we're leaving. And I waited for the morning of the next day, and this time the knapsack was observed. No, it wasn't. So I had to wait till the housewife called us to the midday meal, and tell her then, pointing to what was in the middle of the room:

"I'm afraid I shall have to be leaving today."

"No! Really? Why do you want to go away?" she said.

"Why? Well, don't you think I should?"

"Well, of course—But you might have stayed on a bit longer; the cows will be going out to spring pasture now, and we should have had more milk."

That was all we said about it, and then she went back to her work.

Bravo, Fru Ingeborg. You're true-blue. It struck me then, as it had done already on several occasions, that she had grown very like Josephine at Tore Peak, both in her way of thinking and her mode of expression. Twelve years of school had laid no foundations in her young mind, though it had loosened much that was firm within her. But that did not matter, as long as she kept a firm hold now.

Nikolai is going down to the trading center, and since he will be bringing back some sacks of flour, he intends to drive. I know very well that I ought to go with him, because then I could catch the mail packet next day but one. I explain this to Nikolai and pay my bill. While he is harnessing the horse, I finish packing my bag.

Oh, these eternal journeys! Hardly am I settled in one place than I am again unsettled in another—no home, no roots. What are those bells I hear? Ah, yes—Fru Ingeborg lets the cows out. They are going to pasture for the first time this spring, so that they shall give more milk.... Here comes Nikolai to tell me he is ready. Yes, here is the knapsack....

"Nikolai, isn't it a bit early to let the cows out?"

"Yes, but they're getting restless in the cow houses."

"Yesterday I was in the woods and wanted to sit down, but I cannot sit in the snow. No, I cannot, though I could ten years ago. I must wait till there is really something to sit on. A rock is good enough, but you can't sit on a rock for very long in May."

Nikolai looks uneasily at the mare through the window.

"Yes, let's go.... And there were no butterflies, either. You know those butterflies that have wings exactly like pansies—there weren't any. And if happiness lives in the forest, I mean if God himself— well, He hasn't moved out yet; it's too early."

Nikolai does not reply to my nonsense. After all, it is only the incoherent expression of a vague feeling, a gentle melancholy.

We go outside together.

"Nikolai, I'm not going."

He turns around and looks at me, his eyes smiling good-humoredly.

"You see, Nikolai, I think I have got an idea; I feel exactly as though an idea had come to me that may turn into a great, red-hot iron. So I mustn't disturb myself. I'm staying."

"Well, I'm very glad to hear that," says Nikolai. "As long as you like being here...."

And a quarter of an hour later, I can see Nikolai and the mare trotting briskly down the road. Fru Ingeborg stands in the yard with the boy on her arm to watch the gamboling calves.

And here stand I. A fine old specimen, I am!

Nikolai returned with my mail; quite a little pile had accumulated in the past few weeks.

"I thought you're not in the habit of reading your letters," said Fru Ingeborg banteringly. Nikolai sat listening to us.

"No," I returned. "Just say the word, and I'll burn them unread."

Suddenly she turned pale; she had put her hand with a smile on the letters, brushing my hand as she did so. I felt a great ardor, a moment's miraculous blood heat, more than blood heat—only for a moment—then she withdrew her hand and said:

"Better read them."

164

She was deeply flushed now.

"I saw him burn his letters once," she explained to Nikolai. Then she found something to do at the stove, while she asked her husband about his journey, about the road, whether the mare had behaved well—which she had.

A minor occurrence, of no importance to anyone. Perhaps I should not have mentioned it.

A few days later.

The weather has grown warm, my window is open, my door to the living room is open, all is still; I stand at the window looking out.

A man entered the courtyard carrying an unshapely burden. I could not see his face very well, but thought it was Nikolai carrying something, so I went back to my table to work again.

A little later I heard someone say "Good morning" in the living room.

Fru Ingeborg did not return the greeting. Instead, I heard her ask in loud, hostile tones:

"What do you want?"

"I've come to pay you a visit."

"My husband isn't in—he's in the field."

"Never mind."

"I do mind," she cried. "Go away!"

I don't know what her face looked like then, but her voice was gray— gray with tears and indignation. In a moment I was in the living room.

The stranger was Solem. Another meeting with Solem. He was everywhere. Our eyes met.

"I think you were asked to leave?" I said.

"Take it easy, take it easy," he said, in a kind of half-Norwegian, half-Swedish. "I trade in hides; I go round to the farms buying up hides. Have you got any?"

"No!" she cried out. Her voice broke. She was completely distracted, and suddenly dipped a ladle into a pot that was boiling on the stove: Perhaps she was on the point of flinging it at him....

At this juncture, Nikolai entered the house.

He was a slow-moving man, but his eyes suddenly quickened as he took in the situation. Did he know Solem, and had he seen him coming to the farm? He laughed a little. "Ha, ha, ha," he said, and went on smiling—left his smile standing. It looked horrible; he was quite white, and his mouth seemed to have stiffened in a smiling cramp. Here was an equal for Solem, a sexual colleague, a stallion in strength and stubbornness. And still he went on smiling.

"Well, if you haven't any hides—," said Solem, finding the door. Nikolai followed him, still smiling. In the yard he helped Solem raise his burden to his back.

"Oh, thank you," said Solem in an uncomfortable tone. The bale of furs and skins was a large one; Nikolai picked it up and put it on Solem's back, swung it to his back in a curious fashion, with needless emphasis. Solem's knees gave way under him, and he fell on his face. We heard a groan of pain, for the paved yard was hard as the face of the mountain. Solem lay still for a moment, then he rose to his feet. His face had struck the ground in falling, and the blood was running down into his eyes. He tried to hoist his burden higher up his back, but it remained hanging slack. He began to walk away, with Nikolai behind him, still smiling. Thus they walked down the road, one behind the other, and disappeared into the woods.

Well, let us be human. That fall to the ground was bad. The heavy burden hanging down so uncomfortably from one shoulder looked bad.

Indoors I heard a sound of sobbing; Fru Ingeborg was in a state of collapse in a chair. And in her condition, too!

Well, give it time—it will pass off. Gradually we begin to talk, and by asking her questions, I force her to collect herself.

"He—that man—that beast—oh, you don't know how dreadful he is—I could murder him. He was the one—he was the first, but now he's getting it all back, he's getting more than his own back—you'll see. He was the first; I was all right till then, but he was the first. Not that it meant a great deal to me; I don't want to seem any better

166

than I am—it was all the same to me. But afterward I began to understand. And it drew so much evil in its train, I fell so low; I was on my knees. It was his fault. And afterward it all grew clear to me. I want that man to leave me alone; I don't ever want to see him again. That's not unreasonable, is it?—Oh, where's Nikolai? You don't think he'll do anything to him, do you? They'll put him in prison. Please, run after them, stop him! He'll kill him—"

"No, no. He has too much sense. Besides, he doesn't know, does he, that Solem has done anything to you?"

She looked up at me then.

"Are you asking on your own account?"

"What do you mean?—I don't understand—"

"I want to know if you're asking on your own account! Sometimes you seem as though you were trying to find me out. No, I haven't told my husband. You can think what you please about my honesty. I've only told him part of it, just a little—that the man wouldn't leave me alone. He's been here once before; he was the man Petra wanted to admit that I wouldn't have in. I said to Nikolai, 'I won't have that man coming in here!' And I told him a little more. But I didn't tell him about myself; so now what do you think of my honesty? But I don't want to tell him now either; I don't ever want to tell him. Why? Well, I don't owe you any explanation. But I don't mind your knowing—yes, I want to tell you, please! You see, it's not because I'm afraid of Nikolai's anger, but of his forgiveness—I couldn't bear to go on living as though nothing had happened. I'm sure he'd try to find excuses for me, because that's his nature; he's fond of me, and he's a peasant, too, and peasants don't take these things so seriously. But if he did find excuses for me, he wouldn't be much good, and I don't want him to be no good; I swear I don't—I'd rather be no good myself! Oh, we both have faults to forgive in each other, but we need all of what's left. We don't want to be animals; we want to be human beings, and I'm thinking of the future and our children.... But you oughtn't to make me talk so much. Why did you ask me that?"

"All I meant was that if Nikolai doesn't know, then it couldn't occur to him to kill the man, and that was what you were worried about. I just wanted to reassure you."

"Yes, you're always so clever; you turn me inside out. I wish now I hadn't told you—I wish you didn't know; I should have kept it to myself till I died. Now you just think I'm thoroughly dishonest."

"On the contrary."

"Really? Don't you think that?"

"Quite the contrary. What you've told me is absolutely right, entirely true and right. And not only that—it's fine."

"God bless you," she said, and began to sob again.

"There now, you mustn't cry. Here comes Nikolai walking up the road as good and placid as ever."

"Is he? Oh, thank God. You know, I haven't really any fault to find with him; I was too hasty when I said that. Even if I tried to find something, I couldn't. Of course he uses expressions sometimes—I mean he says some words differently, but it was only his sister that put that into my head. I must go out and meet him now."

She began to look around for something to slip over her shoulders, but it took her a few minutes because she was still quite shaken. Before she had found anything, Nikolai trudged into the yard.

"Oh, there you are! You haven't done anything rash, have you?"

Nikolai's features were still a little drawn as he replied:

"No, I just took him over to see his son."

"Has Solem got a son here?" I asked.

Neither of them replied. Nikolai turned to go back to his work, and his wife went with him across the field.

Suddenly I understood: Sophie's child.

How well I remember that day at Tore Peak, when Schoolmistress Sophie Palm came in to tell us the latest news about Solem, about the bandage on his finger, the finger he never had time to get rid of—stout fellow! They made each other's acquaintance then, and probably met again later in the town. Solem was everywhere.

The ladies at the Tore Peak resort—well, Solem was no angel, but they did little to improve him. And so he met this woman who had learned nothing but to teach....

168

I ought to have understood before this. I don't understand anything any more.

But something has happened to me now.

At last I'm beginning to suspect that their chief reason for wanting to keep me here is simply that they need money; my board and rent are to pay for the mare. That's all it amounts to.

I should have known it long ago, but I am old. Perhaps I may add without being misunderstood that the brain withers before the heart. You can see it in all grandparents.

At first I said "Bravo!" to my discovery, "Bravo! Fru Ingeborg," I said, "you are priceless once again!" But human nature is such that I began to feel hurt. How much better it would be to pay for the mare once and for all and depart; I should have been more than pleased to do so. But I should not have succeeded. Nikolai would have shaken his head as though it were a fairy tale. Then I began to calculate that in fact there couldn't be much to pay for the mare now—perhaps nothing, perhaps she was paid for....

Fru Ingeborg labors and slaves—I'm afraid she works too hard. She seldom sits down, though her pregnancy is far advanced now and she needs rest. She makes beds, cooks, sees to the animals, sews, mends, and washes. Often a lock of gray hair falls down on either side of her face, and she is so busy that she lets it hang; it's too short to be fastened back with a pin. But she looks charming and motherly, with her fine skin and her well-shaped mouth; she and the child together are sheer beauty. Of course I help to carry wood and water, but I make more work for her just the same. When I think of that, I grow hot about the ears.

But how could I have imagined that anyone would want to keep me for my own sake? I should not have had all these years too many then, and these ardors too few. A good thing I've found it out at last.

In a way the discovery made it easier for me to leave them, and this—time when I packed my knapsack, I meant it. But at least the child, her boy, had some love for me, and liked to sit on my arm because I showed him so much that was strange. It was the child's instinct for the peerless grandfather.

At about this time, a sister of Fru Ingeborg's came to the farm to help with the housework. I began to pack then; overcome with grief,

I packed. To spare Nikolai and the mare, I decided to make my way down to the steamship landing on foot. I shall also arrange to relieve all of us of the need for farewells and handshakes and au revoirs, believe me!

But in spite of my resolution, I could not, after all, avoid taking them both by the hand and thanking them for their hospitality. That was all that was necessary. I stood in the doorway with my knapsack already on my back, smiling a little, and behaving splendidly.

"Yes, indeed," I said, "I must begin to move about again."

"Are you really going?" said Fru Ingeborg.

"Why not?"

"But so suddenly?"

"Didn't I tell you yesterday?"

"Yes, of course, but—would you like Nikolai to drive you?"

"No, thank you."

The boy was interested now, for I had a knapsack on my back and a coat with entirely unfamiliar buttons; he wanted me to carry him. Very well, then—just for a moment. But it was for more than a moment, more than a few moments, too. The knapsack had to be opened and investigated, of course. Then Nikolai entered the room.

Fru Ingeborg said to me:

"I'm afraid you think that just because my sister's here now—but we've got another room. And besides, now that it's summer, she could easily sleep in the loft."

"But, my dear child, I must leave some time—I have work to do, too, you know."

"Well, of course," said Fru Ingeborg, giving it up.

Nikolai offered to drive me, but did not press me when I thanked him and refused.

They came to the gate with me, and watched me walk away, the boy sitting on his mother's arm.

At the bend of the road, I turned round to wave—to the child, of course, not to anyone else—only to the child. But there was no longer anyone there.

XXXVIII

I have written this story for you.

Why have I written thus? Because my soul cries out with boredom before every Christmas, boredom with all the books that are all written the same way. I had even the intention of writing in dialect, so as to be truly Norwegian; but when I saw you understood the country's language also, I gave up writing in dialect because, for one thing, it is becoming obsolete.

But why have I gathered so many incongruities within a single framework? My friend, one of the most celebrated literary creations was written during a plague, because of a plague—this is my answer. And, my friend, when you have lived for a long time away from the human beings you know inside and out, then you indulge once more in the iniquity of speech; your powers have been so little used that your head is filled with a thousand sermons. This is my defense.

If I know you at all, you will revel in one or other of my outspoken passages; especially where there is a nocturnal episode, you will lick your chops. But to others you will shake your head and say: "Think of his writing such things!" Alas, small, vulgar soul, retire into solitude and try to understand that episode! It has cost me much to surrender it to you.

Perhaps, too, you will be interested in myself and ask about my irons? Well, I may give you their greeting. They are the irons of one who is half a century old—he has no other kind. But the distinction between myself and my brother travelers is that I freely admit: I have none but these. They were planned so big and so red; yet they are small irons, and they hardly glow. This is the truth. They congregate with the painstaking works of others round the Christmas table. This is the truth. It is the truth even though, in spite of everything, they are distinct from the nothingness of others.

171

You cannot judge this, for you are the modern spirit in Norway, and this is the spirit I scorn.

One thing you will admit: you have not wasted your time in "cultured company"; I have not tried to quench your little upstart heart with a "lady." I have written about human beings. But within the speech that is spoken, another lies concealed, like the veins under the skin, like a story within a story. I have followed the septuagenarian of literature step by step, and reported the progress of his disintegration. I should have written this description long ago, but I had not years enough; only now am I entering upon them, directly and indirectly. I should have done it while the country was groping for long periods under the shadow of superannuated incompetence. Instead I do it now, when I myself am being accused of a tendency to cast shadows. "Sensationalism," you will say, "chasing after fame!" My dear, chaste friend, I have fame enough for the last twenty years of my life, and after that I shall be dead. And you? May you live long; you deserve it. May you almost survive me—in the flesh.

I have just read what a man on the pinnacle of culture has said: "Experience shows that when culture spreads, it grows thin and colorless." Then one must not raise an outcry against the bearers of a new renaissance. I can no longer herald a renaissance; it is too late now. Once, when I had the power to do much and the desire to do more, mediocrity everywhere was too strong. I was the giant with the feet of clay—the lot of many youths. But now, my small, small friend, look about you: there has appeared, within even your field of vision, a figure here and a figure there, a shining crest, lavish with its bounty, geniuses beneath the open sky—you and I should bid them welcome. I walk in the evening of life and, trembling, recognize myself in them; they are youth with jeweled eyes. Yet you begrudge them your recognition; yes, you begrudge them fame. Because you are nobody.

To you—to the modern spirit of Norway! I have written this during a plague, and because of the plague. I cannot stop the rot; no, it is unassailable now, it flourishes under national protection, tarara-boom-de-ay. But one day no doubt it will stop. Meanwhile I do what I can to fight it; you do the reverse.

Of course I have shouted in the marketplace; perhaps that is why my voice is hoarse now, cracked at times. There are worse things. A worse thing would have been if it had not obeyed me. Is there any danger of that? No, my friend, not for you; you will live till you die, be assured.

Why have I written to you, of all people? Why do you think? You refused to be convinced of the truth and integrity of my conclusions; but I shall yet force you to recognize that I am close to the truth. Not until then shall I make allowance for the fool in you.